SAVED BY WOLVES

A BOUND TO THE FAE NOVEL

EVA CHASE

Eva C

Saved by Wolves: A Bound to the Fae Novel

First Digital Edition, 2022

Copyright © 2022 Eva Chase

Cover design: Knesart - Book Cover Designs

Ebook ISBN: 978-1-998752-02-7

Paperback ISBN: 978-1-998752-07-2

1

Kara

*E*very true-blooded fae dreams of the day they'll meet their soul-twined mate, the love that fate has chosen for them. When my parents talked about what I'd experience when it was my turn, it was always something absolute. A knowing right down to the very core of your being, tearing you open with the awareness that your mind, heart, and soul would never be alone again. Connecting you unshakeably to the thoughts and feelings of the truest partner any being could have.

It's the most precious of the gifts offered to the few of us who've stayed dedicated to our heritage rather than mixing with humankind like the diluted fae we rule over.

And every true-blooded fae has received that gift... except for me.

Of course, finding my mate was the farthest thing

from my mind that day when I walked with my parents toward the arch-lord who'd stopped by the refugee camp to check on us. Our flock of raven-shifting Unseelie had just been forced to evacuate our village along the frigid fringes of the Mists in the face of an attack by the Murk, the scheming outcast rat shifters who wanted to steal the winter realm for themselves.

Even in the best of situations, I wouldn't have expected the bond to appear anytime soon. I hadn't even seen out my first century of life yet. Many true-blooded fae didn't connect with their soul's partner for two or three hundred years—or even more.

Arch-Lord Corwin was standing amid a few other lesser Unseelie lords who'd come to thank him for his help. The sunlight glancing off the snowy landscape made his bronze-brown skin look polished and caught on the blue tones in his glossy black curls. I imagined his feathers must be the same shade when he shifted.

At his side, his unusual soul-twined mate—the one I'd heard others refer to as Lady Talia—clutched a basket in front of her. Her pink and purple hair stirred with the cool breeze as she offered the contents of the basket to the lord ahead of us, who picked out a few pastries to bring back to his flock.

I knew the hue in her hair was an illusion, though. She wasn't true-blooded; she wasn't even fae. She couldn't transform into a raven like even the lowliest of our own Unseelie kind or a wolf like the Seelie across the border in the summer realm. Somehow one of the highest Unseelie rulers had found himself bound to a human woman.

In that moment, their presence was only a curiosity—

and a reason to be nervous. I hadn't seen an arch-lord since the one in front of us made the rounds after his coronation, decades ago. Our flock was a lowly one, rarely involved in any business important enough to bring us here to the domains around the Heart at the center of the Mists.

Beneath the plateau that held the homes of the five arch-lords, the pulse of the Heart's energy resonated through my body, so much more potent than the faint whispers I'd sensed of it back home. What would it be like to live right next to the immense, glowing mass of power that granted all fae their magic and kept life thriving throughout the Mists? I couldn't even imagine.

I jerked my thoughts away from those daydreams when it was our turn to approach the arch-lord and focused on him instead. Distant as our flock was from the prestigious pinnacle of the winter realm, we still had our pride. I'd like to stretch my wings more, both figuratively and literally, and I'd hate to embarrass myself in front of someone so important. Someday I'd be lady of our flock myself.

Father stepped ahead of Mother and me and inclined his head in a respectful bow. As he assured Arch-Lord Corwin and Lady Talia that they'd already been generous enough, my gaze lingered on the arch-lord.

He must have had his hands full with the unexpected invasion by the rats, but he was concerned enough about his people to come down to the camp and speak to us face-to-face. Would the other arch-lords do the same?

That question was just flitting through my mind when

Arch-Lord Corwin's attention moved to me. Our eyes met —and a jolt of electricity blazed through my nerves.

My body tensed automatically. The impact of our connected gazes resonated through every part of my body. My breath snagged in my throat, and I braced myself for more—for the flood of sensations that were supposed to overwhelm me as his awareness melded with mine. An ache formed down the center of me from throat to gut.

No recognition sparked in the arch-lord's eyes. A frown touched his lips, and he glanced around as if puzzled. I couldn't wrench my gaze away from him.

Why wasn't he reacting like I was?

My thoughts whirled in my head. I couldn't hear anything but the thudding of my heart. I stared into his uncertain eyes, searching for an answer that every particle of my being knew should be there.

The words tumbled from my mouth. "I— Can't you feel it?"

Arch-Lord Corwin's frown deepened. "I'm sorry. I can't say I understand what you're referring to."

That was impossible. He should sense it just as deeply as I did. That was how it *always* happened, the way everyone told it.

I didn't know what to say, how to articulate the crackling, pulsing impression that had taken over my chest. "I—you—" My hand rose to press against the sharpest point of the ache inside. "*I* can feel it. You're my soul-twined mate."

"What?" a voice burst out, and suddenly I was aware of the other people around us again. Of the human woman with the pink-and-purple hair who was now gaping at me from next to the arch-lord—next to my fate-given mate...

The woman Arch-Lord Corwin had already taken as *his* soul-twined mate. How could she be that to him when I knew I was meant to be? None of this made any sense.

But the ache within me wasn't opening up with trickles of Corwin's consciousness. The bond wasn't solidifying between us. I could feel it straining, trying to catch hold of the being at the other end of our fated connection... and failing.

Concern tightened the arch-lord's face, but it was the palest of echoes of the agony spreading through my body.

"I'm sorry," he said. "There may be an explanation for this. It hadn't occurred to me to think... I'll have to consult with my advisors about what might be done for you. But I can't be your mate—my soul is already twined."

The firmness of his last sentence cut me to the bone. His tone was cool and steady with no room for argument despite the turmoil raging inside me.

I looked at the woman whose hand he'd just taken— the human woman who had no business forming any kind of magical bonds at all—and something twisted low down in my belly. A taste like ashes coated my tongue.

I didn't care what explanation there could be. I didn't want anything to be done other than for my intended mate to meet my gaze with the same longing that thrummed through my veins.

She was the barrier between us, the obstacle who'd pushed her way into the spot meant for me. She'd stolen the deepest of loves that should have been mine without a care that I could never have another.

A flame lit inside me, searing enough to burn away a little of the pain. It made me feel stronger, steadier. So I opened myself up to it, letting it eat away at the edges of my agony and assure me that I hadn't lost this battle yet.

The scorching sensation tickled through every inch of my body until there wasn't a shred of me that didn't hate her.

2

Ten years later

Kara

A frigid wind whips across the icy expanse beyond my parents' castle. I close my eyes against it and murmur the last few words to fortify the carriage I've conjured.

It's a small one, only meant to carry me and modest supplies. I don't want anything that'll draw attention—well, any more attention than an Unseelie craft traveling through the summer realm will draw simply by virtue of existing. Although perhaps the Seelie are more used to seeing ravens passing through now that the fae are mingling more often in the recent peace.

I wouldn't know. I haven't been allowed to set foot outside my desolate fringe domain for the past ten years as I did my penance for my crimes.

Opening my eyes to view the finished carriage, I shake those thoughts away. I'm moving forward now, pushing onward into a new life. Which thankfully includes leaving Hazeleven, my home of nearly a century, behind.

The vehicle may be small, but I can't see any flaws to it. The dark wooden hull curves smoothly to avoid catching the wind, and I've added a small canopy in the summer style to prepare for the blazing sun I expect to find on the other side of the Mists.

I let out my breath with a brief flash of satisfaction and pick up my bundles of food and clothes to set them by the stern behind the single seat.

Footsteps tap across the frozen earth. I know without glancing over that it's my parents. They come up beside the bow of the carriage, my father's face tense and paler than usual, my mother clasping her hands tightly in front of her as if straining to hold on to something that's slipping through her fingers.

She speaks first. "Are you really sure? Even with the peace treaty, some of the wolves still resent us. And you never know when their savagery might come out."

"You have the whole of the winter realm to travel around in if you simply want to see more of the world," Father puts in.

We've already had this argument at least ten times since I got back from my hearing—the hearing with the arch-lords where I was granted an almost total release from my sentence. I'm tired of the debate.

"Almost the whole," I say with an edge in my voice. "Not the domains around the Heart."

Both of my parents stiffen at the reminder that I'm still considered a threat to our rulers. I'm not sure how much they really want me to stay and how much they simply feel it's their duty as parents to caution me against a course of action *they'd* never take. But they're not me, and they're not in my position.

They didn't have to get down on their knees like a beggar as I did to prove my repentance. And not just in front of the arch-lords but a human as well.

Lady Talia.

The next flash of emotion that shoots through me has a sharp edge to it, but I shake that off too. Jealousy and anger are what dragged me down to begin with. I shamed myself and my family. My parents should be glad I'm leaving.

But I can't totally snuff out the prickle of resentment. She hasn't even given Arch-Lord Corwin an heir yet, I've heard. Too busy producing wolves and rats with the other lovers he tolerates. I'd have dedicated myself to him and him alone— I'd have—

My hands clench at my sides. I force myself to inhale and exhale slowly, willing the flare of anguish away. I'm moving on from that emotion too. The woman I became in the grips of my rage isn't someone I'd ever have wanted to be. I'm leaving her behind farthest of all.

I *have* left her behind. It's just having so recently seen the man who was supposed to be mine and the woman he bound himself to instead has stirred up those long-dormant emotions. They'll fade again like they did before.

Like the bond itself has. Not even a slight pang still stirs in my chest marking the failed connection. Over the past decade, it dwindled and then guttered out like a candle burned down to the base. I don't know if it could rekindle even if Arch-Lord Corwin's soul were suddenly free to twine with mine after all.

And that's for the best.

"I need a total change in scenery," I go on, meeting my mother's and then my father's eyes. "A chance to figure out what my life is going to be from now on without any expectations."

I'm not getting the story they always told me where I'd be showered with the great love of a soul-twined mate and a new domain to call home. I need to write a new tale for myself.

A few of our flock-folk glide toward the village around the castle on a larger carriage of their own. They cut their glances toward me and away again, their voices falling to a murmur. An itch ripples over my skin with the urge to ruffle feathers I don't have out.

I need to figure out what my life is going to be someplace away from all my fellow Unseelie who see me as something a hundred times worse than a simple criminal. Everyone in the winter realm knows what I did, the near-catastrophe I set in motion.

The Seelie had their own traitors to focus on during the war. My name won't spark the same recognition there.

I drop the last parcel into the carriage, abruptly twice as impatient to get on with my departure. Then I grab Mother and Father each in a quick hug, ignoring the faint ache around my heart at how woodenly they return it.

"I'll send word every week or two so you know I'm all right," I say, although I'm not sure they wouldn't rather pretend I no longer exist once I'm out of their sight.

"Be careful," Mother says, in words that sound rehearsed rather than heartfelt. "We'll miss you."

More of the flock have come out of their houses in the village to help unload the larger carriage, and the dark glances aimed my way have me leaping into my carriage without another word. The sooner I'm away from all those accusing stares, the better.

But as I open my mouth to speak the true name that will set the craft in motion, one of the castle's staff comes hustling out. "Lady Kara! Can you hold off a moment?" She lowers her voice as she reaches us. "Your grandfather woke up in a bad way—he's calling for you."

I hesitate, which makes the guilt already rising up inside grip me twice as hard. Grand-da was the only reason I didn't leave the second I got home from my hearing. I took the last few days mostly to go over the best techniques for calming him when he gets into one of his states with a few of the flock-folk.

It's me he's used to, though. My affinity magic of the nerves has meant I've always been the one who could soothe his panics the easiest. And he's repaid me more than enough with the stories he'd tell and affection he'd offer during the saner periods in between.

He's the only one here in Hazeleven I'm sure will really miss me—and I'm going to miss him too.

A lump fills my throat. So, even though I'm aware of the flock-folk watching this conversation and probably hoping I'll be gone from their sight soon, and even though the longing to escape this place and their judgment is wrenching at me, I clamber out of the carriage again. "I can stay a little longer."

I find Grand-da in his room, pacing and muttering to himself in urgent tones about something to do with "the beasts." He used to go along the border territories and fend off the feral creatures that stalk us fae when they see their chance. One of those beasts bashed him hard across the head before he could kill it, and his mind hasn't been totally right since then. He often wakes up thinking he's surrounded by dozens of monstrous foes.

Instinctively, I touch the spot just above my hip where the arcing symbol for nerves marks my skin. It formed there automatically, like a dark tattoo springing out of my flesh, when I fully mastered the true name that would allow me to harness this one aspect of our world. Someday I may have learned so many that they spiral out as far as my jaw and temples like they do on the most aged and studious of the fae.

Like they do on the man in front of me.

The syllables spill from my lips with the ease of practice. "*Trin-vie-sum-dal.*"

With the recitation of the true name, a starker awareness of my grandfather's frayed emotional state ripples through me. "It's all right, Grand-da," I add, walking up to him, channeling the magic I've drawn on into my voice. "They're all gone now. You're safe here with your family."

As he turns to face me, I focus on my sense of the anxiety thrumming through his body. Speaking the true name again, I will the racing of his heart to slow and the adrenaline flooding him to taper off.

My own nerves tingle with the beginnings of fatigue, but I'm going to do this right while I'm still here. No cutting corners.

Grand-da's wizened face relaxes. The sight sends a rush of relief through me. He pats my cheek with the brilliant smile that makes me feel like I *am* more than a criminal and a traitor, and I pull him into a firmer hug than I offered my parents.

"You said you were going on a trip, Kara," he says as he hugs me back. "I hope I didn't interrupt it."

"No, not at all," I say, just shy of an overt lie. "I hadn't left yet. It's good to see you one last time."

———

When I send my first message back to Hazeleven from the summer realm a week later, imbuing a little magic in a leaf that will flit its way to my parents, I summon my memory of Grand-da's smile. It's the last real smile I've gotten.

I lean back against the side of my carriage, which is still holding up after a week of drifting through the Seelie side of the Mists, and look toward the pack village I just departed from. The wolf shifters there treated me pretty much the same way as the other packs I've encountered, with wary disinterest. No one's been outright hostile because of my heritage, but no one's been particularly friendly either.

My status as a true-blooded fae, obvious from the sharply pointed tips of my ears, has earned me enough good will that I've been well-fed and offered a guest room in the castles of some of the summer lords and ladies. I can't say I've really felt welcome anywhere, though.

Maybe that was a ridiculous aspiration. We've stuck to our own kind on either side of the border between summer and winter for thousands of years. What could I really have in common with a bunch of hot-headed canines?

It isn't hard to see where their temperament comes from. Even late in the afternoon, with the shadows of the trees around me stretching long, the summery heat hasn't let up. Though I adjusted the charms on my clothes to cool me off rather than warm me up, the humidity clings to my skin and brings out a sheen of sweat on my forehead.

I swipe at it and grimace. A fat bee buzzes by, the sudden sound making me flinch. The pungent scents of the vegetation around me are nearly as overwhelming as the weather.

Would I really want to set down roots in this glaringly vivid and uncomfortably sticky place? How can the wolves stand it?

I suppose they're used to it and must think our domain is too chilly and subdued. I'm not sure it's better to melt than be frozen.

But there's still nothing I want waiting for me back at home either. At least here, I haven't gotten any glares or glowers. No one's associated me with crimes against the arch-lords and their mate.

Maybe I've simply stuck too close to the fringes. The weather is always harsher there. I can go much farther toward the center of these lands without intruding on the arch-lords' domains that I'm forbidden to enter.

I turn toward the carriage, but the thought of directing it through more patches of forest and stretches of rolling hills makes me restless. I can scout out the terrain around here faster when flying, and I might get a better idea of the most hospitable spots from above. It's been too long since I let out my raven.

I suck in the warm air and will my animal to the surface. As my body contracts, feathers sprout from my skin in place of my clothes. My dress absorbs into me, ready to reappear when I shift back. Wings stretch out where my arms once were. I push off toward the sky with a caw of delight that I can't restrain.

The wind ripples over my newly dynamic form. I flap my wings and soar on one current and another. For several minutes, I simply revel in the freedom of coasting above the forests, knowing I can find my carriage again with a simple spell when I need to.

My sense of escape only lasts so long. The sun is sinking—I won't be able to make out a lot of the terrain below once it's dark. Time to get on with my actual goal.

I fly swiftly over forestlands and fields and a lush marsh full of vivid purple flowers that cast their scent all the way up into the sky. Fae both in human-like and wolf forms move on the ground beneath me, too distant for me to make out much of their expressions.

I pass a keep formed out of massive reeds and another sculpted from clay, then a castle that shines like copper. None of them call to me enough for me to want to stop and investigate further.

Or maybe I'm just procrastinating.

The sun touches the horizon and sets it alight with a golden glow. As I come up on another forest, I drift closer to the treetops to peer between them. Hunger is starting to gnaw at my gut, but a different sort of longing propels me onward. There has to be *some*place I'd want to stay for a little while, where I might feel like I could contribute something worthwhile

I'm just veering to the right when a bolt of light hurtles toward me as if out of nowhere. I have only a split-second to register the whine of the magical energy, its blaze blotting out my vision, before it smacks into my chest.

I tumble to the side, my head reeling, my wings seizing up. Pain splinters through my frame. As I flail to catch my balance, my body whirls around. I can't control my direction, can't slow myself down.

The trunk of a tree rushes at me far too fast. I manage to twist sideways at the last second, but my head still bangs into the bark. My skull rattles with the impact, and my vision hazes.

The last thing I'm aware of as I careen toward the ground is a deep voice shouting out in alarm from somewhere nearby. Then the world goes black.

3

Kara

The pain jabs at my head from multiple directions. It feels as if several naughty fledglings are pinching my scalp with tiny beaks.

A rough noise breaks from my throat. I turn my head, abruptly aware of solid ground beneath me and the tickle of grass against my bare forearms, and propel my eyelids open by what feels like sheer force of will.

"Easy there," a gruff male voice says. My blurred vision wavers and then comes into focus, and my body tenses with the urge to flee.

Three men are poised around me in the dimming evening light. The one who spoke crouches near my head, his expression grim but his dark green eyes oddly intense as if he has some reason to care what happens to me.

Even with the grimness, his face is striking enough to

make me catch my breath. Muscles bulge across his shoulders and down his arms beneath skin the burnished brown of fired clay, etched with the darker lines of his many true names. The tips of his ears poke through his bristly black hair, not as sharply pointed as mine—not true-blooded—but with enough of an angle to indicate his parents must have been close.

The second man kneels near my hip. He flashes a smile when my eyes meet his, bright in his tan face but also sympathetic. He's equally stunning but not as bulky as the first, lankier in frame, but I can tell even in his current position that he's tall. There's a youthful vibe to his pose that makes me suspect he's younger than his companion too. With his smooth chestnut-brown hair pulled back into a short ponytail, the rounded tops of his ears are obvious.

His fae blood is much more faded. And he has fewer true-name marks too, none of them creeping higher than his neck while his gruff companion has a few poking from his hairline and over his jaw.

The third of the bunch stands stiffly upright near my feet like some kind of dark sentinel. Not dark in coloring —everything about that is luminous, from his vivid red hair to his pale skin in sharp contrast with his own many true-name symbols to the piercing eyes that shine like polished maple as they study me. It's his attitude that feels ominous as a storm cloud. He's eyeing me like I'm a potential threat, and the scars that slash across his otherwise well-sculpted face suggest he has plenty of experience at dealing with danger.

My stomach sinks as I take in the scars. I can tell from

the shape and angle that they weren't claw wounds. No, those slashes were dealt by talons raking from above.

Raven talons.

All three of the men wear the loose tunics and casual trousers preferred by the summer fae for everyday wear. Their wolfish scents prickle into my nose. I'm surrounded by Seelie—and at least one of them has ample reason to see a raven as the enemy. My pulse thumps faster. Could one of them be the fae who aimed that searing bolt of magic at me?

"Waking up is a good first step," the lanky, youthful man says with another grin. I don't know how he can sound so cheerful. "How do you feel? Do you remember what happened?"

"I—" My voice comes out ragged. I clear my throat and raise my hand to my head where my skull is still aching.

The brawny man frowns and leans forward with a murmur of a true name, and I stiffen. "What are you doing?"

The cooling sensation already seeping through my scalp gives me my answer before he even speaks, with a deeper frown. "A minor healing spell. You seem to have banged your head badly."

"Nothing looks to be broken, though," his companion adds in the same chipper tone as before.

I want to tell them not to cast any magic on me, to leave me alone, but enough of my sense of propriety is left for me to realize that'd be horribly rude when they appear to be trying to help me. I'd probably look hysterical. And I could probably use a little help. If they're healing me, then it seems unlikely that they're the ones who hurt me.

I knit my brow, trying to piece together exactly how I ended up sprawled on the forest floor in my muddled state. "You found me?"

The cheerful guy nods and motions to the solemn one who cast the numbing spell. "Ronan saw you hit the tree and fall. We wanted to make sure you were okay."

The man whose name is apparently Ronan tips his head in acknowledgment. "You looked as if you'd already been injured in some way before the collision—you were flying erratically right before. Brice was able to seal the cut on your forehead, but I'm not sure if you have other injuries. How do you feel?"

Brice must be the chipper wolf. I turn my head and then shift my limbs carefully, testing for pain. "I've got quite a headache—but it's a little better now. Thank you. I don't think—"

My voice cuts off with a hitch of breath when I twist slightly at the waist and a stabbing sensation shoots through my ribs. The red-haired man standing over me takes a brisk step forward, his expression tightening. Brice lifts his hand to hover over my side.

"You might have cracked a rib or two." He glances over me to Ronan. "You've got a better handle on bone than I do, I think."

Ronan's forehead furrows. "I'll do my best." He aims an apologetic glance at me. "None of us are especially trained in healing."

"That's all right. I appreciate whatever you can do." The Heart only knows what I'd have done if they *hadn't* come to my assistance. I'm not sure how I'd have made it back to my distant carriage with a head wound and broken ribs.

The sense of helplessness sets my pulse off-kilter again. They seem kind, but can I trust that? I didn't expect anyone to fling random attacks at me either. There are obviously villains among the summer fae.

And now I'm in no state to defend myself against them.

But Ronan simply rests a hand lightly on my side and mutters another true name. A brief ache radiates through my side and then fades away. His frown comes back. "I think they're more stable now, but they'll probably still hurt for a while. I couldn't seal the cracks completely."

When he removes his hand, the gesture provokes a strange sense of loss. I'm still nervous, surrounded by these three wolf shifters, but the strength that emanates from them isn't entirely intimidating. There's something kind of... appealing about the way they're hovering over me, the protectiveness they're offering. I'm not sure anyone from my own flock would have run to my rescue like this —not in the past ten years, anyway.

Because my own flock is no longer sure I'd be worth saving. These Seelie don't know who I am. They have no idea what I did to the woman who's a mate to one of their own arch-lords as well as one of the Unseelie's.

If they did, I can only imagine how they'd recoil.

My gut clenches, but the thought of my own past crimes stirs the more recent memory of one committed against me. The reason I careened into the tree to begin with.

I push myself upright, gritting my teeth against the splinters of pain that linger in my torso. My mind spins for a second with a brief throbbing.

I gather my wits enough to ask, "Have you seen anyone else around? I *was* injured already—someone threw a blast of magic at me while I was flying over the forest."

Is my attacker still lurking somewhere nearby, waiting to take another shot at me?

The men exchange a glance. The two crouched on either side of me mostly look puzzled, but my sentinel seems to scowl, as if the question annoys him.

"I haven't scented anyone nearby," he says, his voice brisk and as hard as his expression. "Why would someone want to attack you? Have you provoked a few wolves?"

I can't stop myself from glowering at him. "I've been careful not to impose, let alone provoke, while I've been traveling here. I have no idea why anyone would have taken aim at me, other than maybe they take issue with ravens in general."

That might be the wrong suggestion to make when I'm staring back at a man who's clearly had his own issues with the Unseelie. But it's true. Any of the summer fae would have reason to hate me if they knew about my past, but at the time the magic hit me, I'd been flying for hours. Even the rare Seelie who might recognize my face and associate it with my crimes wouldn't be able to identify me from my raven form.

He's definitely scowling now. "We respect the treaty and the peace."

Ronan raises his eyebrows. "But not everyone does,

Nyle. If she says someone attacked her, chances are it was some resentful mongrel. It isn't as if there are a whole lot of ravens and rats living around here, and I hardly think a tree blasted her."

Nyle the sentinel doesn't bother to even respond to the other man's point. I'm getting the impression that he's guarding the rest of his people from *me* rather than me from them.

"Do you have a name?" he asks.

I restrain a glower and summon the response I've been giving to everyone who's inquired so far. I haven't wanted to give the name of my actual domain in case it sparks a memory for any of my hosts, but it's easy enough to give an answer that obscures it without sounding like a lie.

"I'm Kara, you could say of Pinedrift. But I've left it behind." And I have in a totally literal sense, because that's the domain next to Hazeleven.

Nyle's eyes narrow. "What are you doing in the summer realm at all?"

My voice comes out tart. "I was under the impression that thanks to the treaty and the peace you're obviously aware of, all fae were welcome in all areas of the Mists. I wanted to expand my horizons and see more of the world." I'm not going to mention to him the deeper-seated reasons I wanted to get away from my home.

Brice perks up. "Are you staying with a specific pack in the area? We could get you back to that domain, wherever your things are and whoever you're traveling with. Wouldn't want them to get worried about you."

I brace my hand against the trunk of the tree behind me and heave myself onto my feet, unable to restrain a flinch at the fresh shock of pain that radiates from my side and my skull. "No one to be worried. I was traveling alone. And I was in between stopping points, figuring out where I'd go next. My carriage is fifty or so miles south of here—my things are in it." Not that I have all that much.

Nyle looks me up and down. "You're not in any state to fly back there right now. Especially not if someone's around here waiting to take another shot at you."

Ronan sets a solid hand on my shoulder, setting off a tingling sensation through my chest. His voice carries a ring of authority that tells me at least between these three men, he's the one in charge. "She can come back with us and take whatever time she needs to recover. We have room."

"I can track down her carriage and bring her belongings," Brice volunteers as if he can't think of any task more entertaining.

I open my mouth and close it again with a tightening of my skin. I don't like the idea of being indebted to these strangers, but I don't have a very good argument for refusing their offer.

I don't have anywhere else to go. It *would* be incredibly unwise for me to try to make my way back to my carriage on my own. I don't know the true names of the trees here well enough to shape one of them into a new craft—and even if I did, my unknown attacker would still be a problem.

These are the first summer fae I've encountered who've shown me any real friendliness—well, two of them have, anyway. Maybe the rest of their pack is similarly inclined. Or they might be able to point me toward another community that wouldn't mind adding a raven to their mix, at least temporarily.

"All right," I say, forcing a smile to cover my reluctance. "Thank you—you've already done more for me than I'd have expected."

Brice chuckles. "We'd be some awful brutes if we went leaving injured fae to stumble around in unfamiliar woods. Now let's see about a carriage of our own."

He claps his hands together and then holds them out as he intones the true name I recognize as *earth*. Ronan steps up beside me, watching his companion call up soil from through the forest floor to form into a canoe-shaped vehicle. I blink, realizing I'm staring.

"You don't use trees?" I ask.

"Junipers are more typical," the brawny man says. "But if you've got enough skill, you can make just about anything fly. Brice is very attuned to the earth."

"Nothing wrong with getting a little dirty," Brice remarks, aiming a wink at us over his shoulder.

My cheeks flush despite myself. It doesn't help that his tan face and tall, toned body are undeniably appealing to look at.

I grope for a change of subject. "Is it far to your village?"

Ronan's posture tenses for reasons I can't decipher. "Farther than you should probably walk in your current state. We were out here hunting as wolves—sometimes we prowl pretty far afield."

"Village," I think I hear Nyle scoff to himself. I don't understand that either.

When Brice finishes sculpting his earthen carriage,

Ronan helps me up into it. The others clamber in around me and set it sailing off. It does only feel like a few minutes with the wind washing over me before we're drawing to a halt at the edge of a clearing.

A pretty small clearing. I can't stop my brow from knitting as I ease myself out of the vehicle, my gaze catching on the four buildings that stand there on their own.

Three are huts no larger than the ordinary flock houses in my domain back home. They stand next to a building that's slightly larger but nothing close to a castle in scale. All of them are built from what looks like a mix of mud bricks and bronze detailing, boxy and plain in structure.

Suddenly the men's response to my mention of a village makes more sense. "You... live here on your own?" I venture.

"We like our independence," Brice says in a typical upbeat tone, and leans close. "I'll just need a hair to lead me to your craft."

I'm too distracted to say more than, "Yes, of course." He plucks the hair from the side of my head so deftly I barely feel it and then hops back into his carriage to go off on his new hunt.

I've found three Seelie men living apart from any pack, lordless, mateless... It's rare for ravens to go flock-less, and I thought it was even more so for wolves. Unless they were banished for crimes so awful no other pack would welcome them.

What exactly *have* I stumbled into here?

4

Nyle

I pace from one end of Ronan's sitting room to
the other, the rhythmic rapping of my shoes
against the gleaming metal floor honing my thoughts.
"There's more going on than she's telling us. A raven,
clearly true-blooded, meandering around the summer
realm alone with no real purpose? That's absurd."

Brice shakes his head in bemusement from where he's
sprawled in one of the armchairs. "You suspect everyone of
bad intentions, Nyle. What other reason *could* she have for
being here?"

"How can we know what goes through a raven's head?"
I mutter, and let out my breath in a huff. "Someone had
enough of a problem with her to try to hurt her."

"I found her carriage right in the area where she said it

would be. And I asked after her in the nearest village—she'd stayed the night there, offered her thanks to them with a little help drying the latest haul of fish they'd brought in. No one had much to say about her, but none of what they did say was accusing."

Ronan's lips pull back in a silent snarl where he's standing behind one of the other chairs, his forearms braced on its back. "It's not so hard to imagine that someone who's had a problem with ravens in general might have seen an opportunity and hurled a spell at a stranger, is it? There's plenty of rot among the summer fae."

As all three of us well know. But that's why I can't totally trust my friends' judgment on this matter.

I grimace. "We don't know for sure that it *was* a wolf who attacked her. Maybe she's had questionable dealings with other ravens or even rats who're in our realm as well. If she could have traveled this way, so could any number of other fae."

"It doesn't matter," Ronan growls. "Someone tried to hurt her—tried to kill her. She's done nothing wrong that we know about. We're not going to badger her about it while she's healing."

"She doesn't exactly strike me as a hardened criminal," Brice puts in. His tone is typically flippant, but I can hear the undercurrent of concern.

I can't totally blame him. Kara's face floats up from the back of my mind: her delicately elegant features and pensive brown eyes framed by waves of maroon and burgundy hair. Even without the bruise marking her forehead where he sealed her wound, there'd be a fragility to her that calls to something in me as it does to my friends.

She's got a toughness to her as well, though. Her response to the attack was to pull herself together and try to figure out what had happened, not to break down in tears. And I can tell she's wary of us. Which maybe is fair after the treatment she's recently gotten in this realm, but it also means we can't assume she's giving us the full story about anything.

I stop in my pacing and swivel to face both of them, setting my hands on my hips. "We can't throw caution to the wind just because she's in a bit of trouble we know nothing about. I know you're having your heartstrings tugged, but this isn't anything like Aliffe. And it isn't any of our business."

Perhaps I shouldn't have mentioned our own past troubles that bluntly. Both of the other men tense up, Ronan's expression turning even stormier and Brice's smile souring. But this isn't the kind of situation where I should beat around the bush. If our past is swaying them, they need to be called out on it.

We can't let previous disasters propel us into a new one.

"What does it matter?" Brice asks, his voice more subdued than before but without any rancor in it. "How could she possibly harm *us*?"

"We're lucky we have even the freedom we've still got," I remind him. "Unless you fancy being sentenced to the fringes to carry out endless drudgery for the arch-lords?"

Ronan snorts. "She hardly seems like *that* much trouble."

He glances toward the door—beyond which lies the larger cabin we'd normally use for meetings like this, as well as our meals. We aren't there tonight because we've set up the raven to sleep in its lounge room, with the most privacy we can give her in our diminished version of a village.

Ronan's grim expression softens just a little. The sight pinches at my chest.

Since we left Saplight, he's been somber at best and grouchy at worst. This is the first real sense of purpose he's found. I don't like tearing it down even if logic dictates that we can't take everything about this woman at face value.

Someone needs to protect these two from their heroic inclinations—and from the guilt I know is eating at all of us.

"I think we should be more concerned about whoever blasted her," Brice says, kicking one of his long legs restlessly. "That one is the real trouble."

I can't argue with him there. In fact, I'd meant to get to that subject in a moment myself. I don't like the idea of a fae who's willing to attack on a whim wandering near the small bit of territory we've claimed for ourselves. And if we can find the one who attacked Kara, they can tell us what issue they had with our injured raven.

I nod. "Why don't we sniff around the spot where we found her and see what we can turn up? If there are rats or other ravens with hostile intent roaming nearby, we'll want to know. And if it's a Seelie, perhaps we'll recognize who."

I pause, my own gaze veering toward the common building where our unexpected guest is sleeping. "One of us should stay behind in case she wakes up in distress."

Or tries to pull something sneaky over on us. Or, I suppose, in case her attacker tracks her down here hoping to finish what they started.

Before either of my friends can speak up, I point at Brice. "You stay back. Keep your ears pricked. Ronan and I have the sharpest noses—and you'll do the best at cheering her up if she needs a little coddling."

Brice wrinkles his nose at me, but his lips twitch with a hint of a smile at the same time. He can't deny any part of what I've said. And the last thing I want is Ronan hanging around adding fuel to his protective instincts and whatever attachment he's already formed to this woman.

Technically, Ronan should be making the calls like that. In most matters, we look to him as if he were our lord. But he recognizes my knack for strategy and doesn't bother to push in with his own authority. We're friends before colleagues, after all.

He pushes to his feet and stalks toward the door without hesitation. "Let's get on with it, then. The longer we wait, the colder the trail will get."

I chuckle and nudge him teasingly as I follow him out. "This from the great tracker who once claimed he could sniff either of us out even if we dressed ourselves in dead rats?"

Ronan bumps his shoulder against mine in return, the rumble of his voice casual in its chiding. "Maybe you shouldn't put so much stock in stories made up by braggart whelps."

"Thankfully you've grown into *most* of your claims of impressiveness," I retort, and leap forward to stretch into my wolf form.

Everything sharpens to my canine senses, distant sounds reaching my ears and the faintest scents tickling my nose. I lope toward the site where we found Kara at a swift pace, with Ronan easily matching it.

A strong whiff of raven lingers where she fell, but nowhere else nearby. That makes sense. She was in the air before she was hit, and we took her on the carriage back to our home. If I catch her scent anywhere else nearby, we'll know she was lying about how long she'd been in flight.

Through an unspoken agreement, Ronan and I veer in different directions, noses close to the ground, circling the spot in wider and wider rings. I shoulder through the brush and veer around trees, inhaling the summery forest smells of vegetation in full bloom. No trace of fae presence seeps into my lungs other than brief wafts when I cross the paths my friends and I took when hurrying to help Kara.

Ronan only saw her a few seconds before she smacked into the tree. Who knows how far she'd hurtled in her injured state before that happened? Or from what kind of distance the spell was hurled across?

There's no good in rushing our investigations. The proof will be there if we're patient enough to seek it out.

We've spread out in our circling to a little more than a mile from our starting point when Ronan lets out a bark of summons. I trot over to the place where he's stopped, breathing even more deeply in case I pick up more than he already has.

There's no hint of raven or rat here either. But when I draw up next to my friend, a faint tang of wolf prickles through my senses. I dip my head lower, drinking in as much as I can.

Undeniably Seelie. Male, middle-aged, in good health. That's as much as I can gather from the scent. I don't recognize the specific musk, but then, we aren't exactly close with any of our neighbors. That doesn't mean it *isn't* someone who lives in one of the domains nearby.

Ronan has started following the trail farther away. I join him, but we haven't gone far before the scent fades away. I frown, wandering in a wider ring to see if I can pick it up again, but it's completely vanished.

Ronan straightens up as a man, and I pull my wolf inward as well. He studies the darkened forest around us, his forehead furrowed. "He must have used magic to dispel his scent. But not in that one spot."

I can think of an obvious explanation for that. "He lingered there longer, so there was more to dispel. And he would have wanted to race off quickly after the attack, especially if he heard us coming to Kara's aid. He covered his tracks as he fled but didn't have time to erase all signs that he was ever here."

"We have no idea where he came from, though. You didn't recognize him?"

I shake my head, knowing the question means that Ronan didn't either. Despite all my previous cautioning, a flare of wrath lights in my chest.

Someone attempted murder near our home. One of our own kind attempted to kill a raven who'd been doing nothing more than flying by. Whatever Kara's reasons for being here, I haven't seen any indication that I should doubt that part of her story.

Maybe this time, we can see justice done where it should be.

5

Kara

"Do you want another buttered roll?" Brice asks from the kitchen area that forms one half of the large cabin's eating area. "Or some more cheese? We can't have you going hungry."

He glances over at me so eagerly I feel guilty about declining. The rich flavor of the meat patty I just finished still lingers enjoyably in my mouth, but my stomach is close to bursting.

I rest my hand on my belly. "I don't think I could fit anything else in there. And you really don't have to go to so much trouble."

"It's no trouble," Ronan says from the chair kitty-corner to mine. His voice is abrupt and growly, but emphatic enough to send a shiver through me that isn't exactly unpleasant.

He looks me over as if scanning for signs of further injury, although he already checked my wounds and layered on more spells to heal them when I first got up this morning. "You've been treated badly, but that isn't what we're like."

"And you need food to give you the energy to heal!" Brice declares before digging into the roll he was waving at me. He grins as he chews. "Those ribs might take as long as a couple of weeks to be fully mended. Which is why I'm going to ensure that you have a proper place to yourself instead of being stuck with our common building."

"What?" I say with a strange flash of emotion that's somehow both alarm and excitement. "I'm fine in the lounge room—it was perfectly comfortable—"

He shakes his head as he ambles toward the door. "We could stand to expand our little 'village' here anyway. I haven't really stretched my earth skills in a while. It'll be good practice. You're doing *me* a favor."

"Um," I say, and then he's gone, so I can't really argue any more.

I glance at Ronan, half expecting *him* to argue. Surely the wolves don't really want to set me up in a whole house of my own here. But he's smiling in his slightly feral way. "We're happy to have you here," he tells me. "We'll make sure the one who attacked you doesn't get anywhere near you again."

Apparently I've been adopted. I'd imagined I'd find some kind of home among the summer fae, but I hadn't expected it to be quite like this. Do they think I'm going to stay even after I've healed?

It's hard to say whether the idea makes me more

relieved or nervous. My emotions are a mess today, it seems. Partly because I'm still not sure what to make of these three men and the odd 'village' they've set up here.

And at least one of them isn't sure what to make of me either. Nyle steps out of the common building's lounge room where I was sleeping, the forceful movement of his compact muscular form immediately drawing my attention. I have the sudden suspicion that he was checking my things rather than simply grabbing the bag he's holding off one of the storage shelves. He studies me with his coolly bright eyes.

"We'll ask around with the packs closest by," he says. "I believe we've caught the culprit's scent. One way or another, we'll find whoever's responsible."

There's a dark undercurrent in his voice that suggests a vicious outcome once they do find my attacker. He might be uncertain of my intentions, but he's still determined to punish whoever hurt me.

The portent in his words sends another tingle through my body. When has anyone cared that much about protecting me?

Ronan lets out a gruff sound and stands up. He rests his hand on my shoulder just for a second, long enough to send a rush of heat through my chest before he withdraws it with a jerk as if he assumes it's unwelcome. "You should stay here by our buildings until we've dealt with the mangy cur. Don't venture farther alone."

My skin tightens with the echo of memory his words stir up: the arch-lords ordering me confined to my home domain ten years ago. For a decade, I was trapped with the knowledge that I couldn't set foot beyond its borders without risking further sanction.

If this 'village' became a cage, it'd be an even smaller one.

"I won't do anything stupid," I say, lifting my chin. That's as much of a promise as I'm willing to make. And then, to get them off the subject of where I should or shouldn't go, I ask, "Are there many packs in the area? Are you associated with any of them?"

I know I'm not imagining the tension that resonates through the air with that question. Ronan and Nyle exchange a brief glance; Ronan's mouth has tightened as if he's restraining a scowl.

"There are a few domains close enough that one of their kin could have wandered out this way," Nyle says evenly. "Whatever they think of us, we have a right to ask questions."

"Especially when someone in our care was wounded," Ronan adds, the growl coming back into his voice.

I'm going to take that as a "no" to my second question —and it sounds like they don't expect the packs around here to be all that friendly to them. How exactly did they end up as a trio of lone wolves?

I still don't know what I've gotten myself into. But these two obviously don't want to give me a straight answer.

Ronan pushes away from the table. "We'll get started on that search now. We can hunt for dinner on the way back."

Right, my crashing into their lives yesterday evening interrupted their hunting expedition. A twinge of guilt pierces through my apprehension. "If there's any way I can help around the, er, village, I'm happy to pitch in. My magical affinities aren't especially useful, but I have a decent range of true names mastered."

My hand rises to my neck, where the mark for silver formed on my skin just last year—my most recent acquisition. I might be just shy of my first century, but thirty true names mastered is a good start for that age. Even if I'm strongest with air and nerves, neither of which contribute a whole lot to the daily tasks of any given flock or, I'd imagine, pack.

Ronan frowns. "Don't worry about that. You're our guest. You're recovering. Rest, and let Brice know if you need anything."

He nods to Nyle, and they stride out of the building without another word.

I don't really feel comfortable simply lounging around while they heap me with food and, by the Heart, a *house*. I will not be a burden. So I collect the breakfast dishes that perhaps Brice would normally deal with and work a couple of true names to wash them clean before tucking them away.

Then I venture outside to see what the most easy-going member of this odd trio is doing. If I can get him talking, maybe he'll offer a little more insight into how they ended up here.

Ronan and Nyle have already vanished, no doubt melded into the shadows of the forest as they lope off toward whatever official domains lie nearby. I find the chestnut-haired Seelie man standing near the edge of the clearing several paces beyond the farthest of the existing houses. He's stretching his lean arms over the ground, murmuring under his breath. The soil beneath the patchy grass has already risen into a wall as high as his knees, about ten feet in diameter, packed hard as clay.

I pause in front of the common building, hesitant to disturb Brice while he's working. His intent focus adds more edge to his youthful good looks, sharpening his brow and hardening his jaw. I'd assumed he was around my age, but he could be several decades older. Still younger than his companions, who I'm guessing have at least two if not three centuries under their belts, but hardly a neophyte.

But then, *none* of these three men have experienced everything I have. I'm not some naïve fledgling.

Definitely not so naïve that I can't appreciate the V of Brice's chest that shows where he's loosened the collar of his tunic, planes of sleek muscle dappled with the dark lines of his true-name marks. A wash of heat tickles up my own neck that has nothing to do with the summer warmth.

Before I can decide whether to approach him, Brice summons the earth another few inches higher and then lets his hands fall to his sides with a pleased but tired sigh. A sheen of sweat glints on his tan forehead. He swipes at the back of his neck beneath his ponytail and glances up, catching sight of me.

I propel myself toward him. "You really don't need to do this. It's so much work—"

He waves my concern off with a grin. "Ah, it's not that bad. Don't make me out to be a weakling now."

My cheeks flush. "I didn't mean any insult."

"Of course not. But, you know, we've been discussing

that we could use another building for storage. If you don't end up sticking around for long, we'll still appreciate having it."

He says that "if" so casually, as though it isn't of much importance whether I insert myself into their lives even more than I already have inadvertently. I suppose they might prefer not to have some stranger puttering around in their common spaces anyway. But I don't get the impression that's the main factor on Brice's mind.

"I wish I could help," I say, frowning at the earthen wall. "I don't have that true name. It's not especially useful in the winter realm. We tend to lean more toward rocks, because there's a lot more stone than soil in the ground, especially near the fringes."

Brice cocks his head. "The domain you mentioned—it's on the outer edges?"

I can give the same answer for both the false one I've given him and my true home. "Yes. One of the reasons I wasn't so keen on staying there."

He chuckles. "I've been to the summer version of the fringelands and almost drowned in the humidity. I doubt I'd last five minutes on the winter side."

I twist a strand of hair around my finger. "It's all what you're used to, I guess." Which gives me the perfect opportunity to ask, "What part of the summer realm *did* you grow up in? Not the fringes, clearly. You obviously didn't always live here."

Brice's gaze flickers, suggesting that he isn't all that more comfortable with the subject than his friends are. But he shrugs easily enough and offers me another smile.

"No. We came from a domain pretty close to the Heart, actually."

"Oh." I blink in surprise and study him more closely. "Why did you leave? I can tell it's a sensitive subject, but I'd feel better having some idea."

Maybe it's unfair of me to ask when I'd do anything to avoid telling them the full reason *I'm* here, but Brice doesn't appear to take offense. He exhales slowly, his smile turning crooked.

"It's nothing horrible," he says. "We wouldn't put you in any danger. We just... There was a major misunderstanding around a very fraught situation, and the people who count the most in our former domain *think* Ronan did something horrible. That's his story to tell if he wants to. But Nyle and I weren't going to let him take the burden of banishment on his own."

Is that the full story, or simply Brice refusing to believe the worst of a friend? It sounded as though the neighboring packs don't think highly of these three either. But then, nothing about Ronan's behavior toward me has felt deceptive or threatening. The only one who doesn't seem perfectly content with my presence is Nyle, and the source of his scars could be reason enough for that.

Which just means I need to feel more guilty about deceiving them. Not that I've outright lied about anything. I wouldn't diminish my connection to the Heart that way, knowing how it recoils from deceit. But I haven't been particularly forthright either.

"I'm sorry you all ended up in that situation," I say.

Brice's smile comes back, softer this time. "It's all right. I feel worse for Ronan. I wasn't going to amount to much where we were anyway—nothing I wanted to amount to, at least."

I can relate to that sentiment so well that my stomach knots. Before I have to figure out how to respond, he lifts his hands again. "I'd better get back to work if I'm going to have it ready by tonight. It won't be the prettiest little house ever, but it'll have four walls and a roof—I promise you that much."

I leave him to his task and find ways to keep myself busy. In one of the Seelie villages I stopped in earlier, I pitched in with a few of the pack-kin in gathering wild herbs, and I spot some of the same types along the borders of the clearing. Perhaps these men would appreciate those too.

As I stoop to pluck the leaves, I note a small path leading between the trees behind the main cluster of buildings. A faint bleating carries from that direction, so I guess the men keep some farm animals. I have the feeling Brice won't like me wandering off that far, though.

I can't depend on their hospitality any longer than is necessary. The pain in my ribs has already dulled to a vague ache. When they *aren't* around to see what I'm doing, I'll have to do some scouting of my own.

Ronan and Nyle arrive just as evening is setting in with a boar carcass and no answers about my attacker. We eat pig flesh roasted in the common building's large hearth and flavored with some of the herbs I gathered, others of which Nyle adds to a salad with the same swift efficiency he seems to bring to every task. Then Brice shows off the hut he's finished for me, its rounded roof standing a few feet taller than I do, a wooden door fastened to the entrance and a swath of linen covering the single window.

We cart over my meager belongings and the bed the men assembled for me last night. Then I wait until they've all shut themselves away in their own homes under the dark blanket of night.

When I'm sure I won't be noticed, I tug the curtain away from the pane-less window, call forth my raven, and slip out into the darkness.

6

Kara

$\mathcal{I}$have a vague sense of which direction my attacker struck me from, so I head that way, to the east. With restrained flaps of my wings, I navigate the outstretched branches of the trees, staying beneath the canopy of leaves. Even during the day, no one would be able to see me from a distance as long as I'm within the shelter of the forest. By night, I might as well be just another shadow.

The forest doesn't last forever, though. When I reach a stretch of grassy hills, I dip even lower to soar just a few feet above the ground. The warm wind ripples over me and rustles through the long blades.

Hints of canine scent reach me, but stronger are the tangs of woodsmoke and roasted meat. I follow them until I spot the dancing flames of a bonfire in the distance.

A few dozen small houses that must belong to a pack stand silhouetted at the far end of the field, clustered around a taller shape with a couple of turrets where this pack's lord or lady must live. I can't make out what material it's composed of.

The Seelie of this pack sway and prance around the fire, pausing to grab food and drinks from the tables set up at one end. I suppose this is some kind of party. Sometimes my parents would gather as many of our flock-folk as wanted to attend for food and dancing in the ballroom of our palace, but no one threw themselves around to the music in wild abandon like some of the summer fae I'm watching now.

The Unseelie prefer not to make spectacles of themselves.

A few rows of apple trees form a small orchard on my side of the field. I land on one of the branches and continue to study the partiers for a while. They appear totally immersed in the music a couple of their number are playing on gleaming instruments and in their jovial conversations with each other.

How would they react if I appeared and wandered into their midst? Would one or more of them look at me with hostility?

Even though they're out in the open, I can't help feeling this is a private moment for the pack. I don't see any obvious signs of discontent or aggression. I push off the branch and veer north, leaving them to their enjoyment.

As I fly on, a pinch of pain wakes up in my chest. My

raven ribs are as sensitive as my healing human ribs were. The shift in bodily shape doesn't remove the injury.

As the minutes slip past me, the pinch expands into a deepening ache. I shake my head against the pain with a ruffling of my feathers.

I came to the summer realm to decide my own fate. I'm not letting some wayward Seelie attacker stall me in my tracks.

Finally, I locate another village. The pack living in these buildings have turned in for the night, other than a couple of wolfish forms I notice prowling around the far edges of their territory. They don't notice me at all when I glide overhead beneath the moonless sky.

They also don't notice one of their pack-kin slinking away into the night. I only spot him because of my high vantage point and the brief glint of starlight that catches on a silver streak down the back of his neck through his otherwise dark fur. That wolf melds into the shadows of a dense forest farther east from his village.

Interesting. Where would he be sneaking off to at this late hour, taking care that none of his pack-kin caught him leaving? I swoop after him.

Flying low to the ground, swerving around the brush, I'm able to keep track of his scent trail from a far enough distance that I have no fear he'll realize he's being followed. He lopes along through that stretch of forest and then a marsh of tall reeds where I have to hang farther back. Finally, he vanishes into the woods on the slope of a hill.

The moment he's out of sight, I push my wings harder, ignoring the growing throbbing in my chest. I'm not going to take any pleasure out of the flight back, but I can't deny my curiosity now.

Within the trees, I pick up my target's scent faintly—and then another whiff of wolf, and another—and one of rat. Even more interesting.

The scents all converge onto a common path. As I glide along it, distant voices reach my ears.

I slow again, soaring from one branch to another as I make my way closer rather than flying straight at them. Other smells mingle with those I've already identified: at least a couple more wolves, another rat… and a raven. What is going on here?

As I edge closer, the speakers become easier to make out. "—made any progress?" a man is asking in a raspy voice.

"I think a couple of my pack-kin are starting to come around to our views," a woman answers. "I don't want to push too hard or too quickly. Our lord is definitely committed to the peace."

There's a nasal-sounding snort. "What he wants won't matter if you can sway enough of the pack."

"I laid a couple of traps near different villages," a fourth person speaks up. "Made sure to leave a ratty odor while obscuring it enough so no one can identify me. They won't be feeling friendly after they stumble into those."

Another woman huffs. "It's moving too slowly. We've had *ten years* of this ridiculous treaty now. More acceptance is taking hold the longer we let it be."

I pause on the latest branch I've perched on. I can't see the speakers yet, but I can hear them clearly now, and those words give me all the answer I need.

They're a group of dissidents. Fae who aren't happy about the new peace and want to re-establish the divisions and possibly the hostilities between us.

It's a wonder they're able to collaborate as much as they seem to be with others of different kinds, but they must see it as a necessary evil to achieve a common goal—to allow them never to have to associate with fae outside their own kind again.

A shiver ripples over my skin. I knew there were fae who disagreed with the treaty and held on to old prejudices, but I hadn't realized any had gone as far as forming groups to take concrete steps toward ending it. Someone with that kind of mindset might very well be the type to aim a blast of magic at a random passing raven, wouldn't they?

It's hard to tell from what I've overheard whether this group has been particularly successful in their efforts or merely irritating. The woman who spoke last clearly doesn't think they're accomplishing enough. Do they have bigger plans they're working toward?

A mix of apprehension and curiosity compels me forward. I can't know how I might need to protect myself without knowing what I'm protecting myself from. This group wouldn't approve of *any* raven wandering around in the summer realm.

If I can describe them to my rescuers, maybe the dissidents can be sanctioned before they do anything worse. Ronan will be annoyed that I flew off on my own, but the chance to bring a whole bunch of traitors to justice should offset his frustration. The criminals in this meeting are defying their own arch-lords.

I'd like to think that I would have pulled off my attempt at spy-craft under normal circumstances. There's no reason I should have been spotted. But as I leap onto a closer branch, my healing body betrays me.

A jolt of pain lances from my chest right through my wing. I swerve erratically, and my other wing hits the branch with a soft thump as I land clumsily rather than stealthily.

The dissidents react instantly. I've barely had time to right myself, my pulse hiccupping, when a flurry of whispered true-names rush through the trees. A spell smacks into my branch, the bark of the tree springing up to lock my feet in place before I can take off.

A croak of protest escapes my throat. Fae push through the brush below me. Three faces come into view, hazy in the darkness but the hostility in their expressions unmistakable.

"Show yourself," one man snaps. "Explain who you are and what you're doing here, fast, or you'll lose any chance to."

He's already raising his hands to cast another true name—possibly one that really will end my life. I jerk on the branch and can't budge my feet.

My only chance is shifting. And once they've seen me —the raven with them might recognize my face or my name—

An eerie calm settles over me. Being recognized might actually be a good thing. I have the tools to find out who these people are simply by revealing who *I* am.

As I expand into the shape of a woman, my gut twists.

Just the thought of what I'm about to do makes me queasy.

The bark shatters. I drop onto the ground on my feet, pressing my hand against the tree trunk for balance.

"I want the same things you want," I say—quickly, because I don't know how long they're going to give me to make my case before they decide they're better off disposing of me. The statement is vague enough to not totally be a lie. We must want *some* of the same things, even if those are only food and shelter and some sort of companionship. "I almost stopped the peace before it even happened."

Shame prickles through my veins that I can say that second statement so baldly without it being even close to a lie. More figures appear behind the three who have me hemmed in against the tree. I still can't make out much of their faces. Their scents mingle together in my nose.

"What is that supposed to mean?" one of them demands.

I wet my lips, tuning out the frantic thud of my heart. "There's at least one raven here, isn't there? I'd imagine you've heard of Kara of Hazeleven."

A tall but slightly stooped man leans closer from the back of the bunch. "What about her?"

I spread my arms. "You're looking at her."

My fellow Unseelie shoulders closer, peering at me with deep-set eyes in a wan face. "*You're* Kara of Hazeleven?"

"I'm Kara of Hazeleven," I say, emphasizing every word so they can tell there's no way I'm simply lying by omission. "Have been since the day I was born. I'm the one who nearly rid our world of that human interloper in our arch-lords' midst. There wouldn't be any peace if my plan had worked and Lady Talia had met the fate I intended."

My nausea rises to the base of my throat, but none of my spectators seem to notice anything concerning in my demeanor. One of them sucks in a startled breath. Another lets out a giggle.

Just this once, the horrors of who I once was may work in my favor instead of against me.

The raven's complexion appears to have gotten even more sallow. "How did you end up out here?" he asks in his throaty voice.

I can't be quite so forthright on that subject, but I can say enough that's true to pass for a full answer. "I recently convinced the arch-lords that I've served enough penance, and I wanted to see the results of the treaty on this side of the border. I got the impression there was some discontent in this area, so I sought you out. And I've heard enough of your meeting to confirm I was right."

One of the wolf shifters growls. "Someone's been too bold."

I manage to laugh. "You're trying to disrupt the status quo. You *want* to get noticed, one way or another. So don't be surprised when people do notice, especially the ones familiar with those kinds of tactics."

"I don't like it," someone mutters near the back of the group. My skin is still prickling with the suspicion that my life is far from secure.

Folding my arms over my chest at a cocky angle, I scan the shadowed faces in front of me. "What, is your membership all full up? No room for any additional rebels, even one with more experience than I'd bet any of you has under your belts?"

"Is that what you're looking for?" the woman closest to me asks, with a rough inhalation as if she's taking in my scent. "To join us? This isn't a drop-in social club."

"Of course it's not." I only have to be convincing enough to make sure they'll let me leave alive. "I wouldn't be here if I wasn't willing to contribute." Here being the summer realm, but they can take it to mean this meeting.

One of the Seelie men gives a sharp sweep of his arm, and the group pulls away from me other than a couple who appear to be standing guard, including the man who first threatened me. The others murmur amongst themselves too quietly for me to make out. I lean back against the tree trunk, resisting the urge to fidget.

I am not nervous. I am totally sure of myself. That's what I want them to see, anyway.

I don't know enough yet to identify any of them to an outside party unless maybe I managed to track them down by their homes and recognize them by daylight. A chill washes through me with that thought.

Even if I did that, I don't have any proof of what I've heard, do I? And why should Ronan stick out his neck on the word of a woman he barely knows when he's already been shunned by his own pack?

Not to mention that if I pushed the matter, I wouldn't be able to avoid revealing who I am to my three rescuers. That truth would come out before any other.

Who would believe my story then? They'd probably think I'm simply stirring up more trouble.

But if I ingratiate myself with this group, if I earn a little trust from them, who knows how much I might uncover? Enough to present the arch-lords themselves with solid proof of who's working against them now? Enough to prove to *everyone* that I'm not the Kara of ten years ago anymore; that I support the peace and the people behind it?

That I can do something as heroic as I once was villainous.

A quiver of excitement passes through my nerves, but they jitter at the same time. It sounds like a lovely dream. I should know that dreams don't generally turn into reality.

If I deceive these fae and they realize my real purpose here, I have no doubt they'd murder me. One of them quite possibly already tried to yesterday, when I hadn't done anything to them at all.

The group presses closer again. The Seelie who drew them away speaks up, as if he's some kind of leader.

"Your help might be welcome. We'll see how committed you are. If you found us so easily, I'm sure you can do it again without any guidance from us. This meeting is over. We'll see if you join us for the next one from the start, Kara of Hazeleven."

"Expect to see me there," I say with all the haughty confidence I can summon. But when I step away, the only impulse left in me is the desire to fly far, far away and never look back.

7

Ronan

$\mathcal{I}$ can tell from the tension in the shepherd's stance that he knows who I am. Or at least he's heard the stories about the three men who settled on unclaimed land not far from his domain a few years back.

"Ravens?" he mutters without quite meeting my eyes. He's mainly watching my hands, as if he thinks I might sprout claws and attack him at any second. "Haven't heard of any outside of that settlement a bunch of them set up a few domains away. Nothing good, and no trouble either."

"No one complaining about one passing by that they had an issue with?" I prod, willing down my hackles. He can't help it if he doesn't know the truth about my situation. I need to be sure I've gotten a full answer about the matter at hand.

"Not that I've heard," he says, and turns at a bleat

from one of his sheep. The ram is glowering at another with a shake of its horns.

I could redirect it with a quick intonation, but somehow I don't think this man would appreciate me casting true names on his livestock. And I'd rather not make this visit any more memorable than it already is. I'd prefer if he doesn't mention to anyone else that I was asking around about ravens, in case word gets back to the would-be murderer.

If that menace tries to come at Kara in our makeshift village... My fangs itch in my gums.

I force a smile and bob my head to the shepherd before my reaction can show. He'll think it's directed at him. "Thank you all the same. I'll let you get back to tending to your charges."

He lets out a huff that could be prompted by me or the sheep—it's hard to tell. Possibly both. It doesn't really matter to me.

As I turn away from him, a grimace slips across my face before I leap forward, releasing my wolf.

It would have been a few hours' run to make it all the way out here on foot, but I left my carriage a mile away so I could do some scouting on the ground before I revealed myself to any of the locals. I've had to push farther abroad since yesterday's inquiries. So far, neither Nyle nor I have gotten any sense of particular animosity toward ravens or recognized the scent we got a taste of near our home.

Could it have been a traveler simply passing by on his way to a much more distant destination? We'd never find the culprit then. It would also make it unlikely that he'll ever target Kara again, but that thought doesn't offer as much comfort as it probably should.

I want to track down the miscreant and deal twice as much pain to him as he did to her. Any fae who'll go around lashing out at innocent strangers doesn't deserve to continue living.

Of course, if I deal out justice myself, I know how badly that could go. But I could certainly teach him a wide variety of lessons and then turn him over to the authorities. They might not care for my account of the situation, but Nyle has never been accused of any wrongdoing. He can identify the cur's scent.

When I reach the carriage, I spring over the hull as a wolf before shifting back. I glance at the sun through the trees, gauging its height.

If I head home now, I'll make it there just before evening. The next nearest domain is even farther abroad. I suspect I'll get a warier welcome if I turn up slinking through the night… and I don't really like the thought of leaving our home to just Brice and Nyle to defend for that long, if Nyle has even returned yet.

Our inquiries are starting to feel increasingly pointless anyway. Restraining a growl of frustration, I point the carriage toward our little settlement and set it flying as fast as it will go.

Maybe my impatience gives my magic an extra rush of energy. The vessel careens between the trees and across open fields, and I catch the familiar scents of what's now *our* forest before the sun has quite reached the horizon.

As I urge the craft the last few miles toward home, a knot forms in my chest. I've been gone for the entire day.

Who knows what could already have happened in my absence? Was asking around the wrong choice—should I have stayed close to Kara to watch over her?

The tension unwinds with a wisp of her cool, dark scent that laces the air—fresh and without any taint of violence. She's all right.

I stop the carriage at the edge of the clearing, dismiss it back into the juniper tree it was formed from, and prowl between the buildings in search of her so I can confirm her safety with my own eyes.

I didn't spend centuries training under my father for nothing. My feet pad across the firmly packed earth so silently that I don't disturb our guest at all.

She's in the garden between my house and Brice's, crouched between two rows of vegetables, her back to me. The fading sunlight brings out the spectrum of colors in her reddish-brown hair, like every sort of wood from cherry to mahogany woven together and polished to a shine.

She's murmuring something under her breath in her soft, smooth voice. For a second, as I pause to watch her, I think she's singing to herself. Then I see her raise her hand with a fluffy seed from one of the fallowroot plants gliding around it, and realize she's speaking a true name. The one for air, sending the seed twirling on a gust of breeze like a dancer.

She calls up another and another until a dozen of them are spiraling around each other like elegant ladies at a ball. The kind of revel she's missing from wherever she came from? Her lordly parents must have held some kind of formal gatherings, I'd imagine, although I don't have much idea how raven revels compare to wolfish ones.

I start to feel awkward simply standing here staring at her. Gaping like a stalker isn't going to make her feel more welcome.

I step forward, clearing my throat. "You have excellent control."

Kara's head twitches around with a tumble of her dark waves. Her fingers curl toward her palm, and the seeds disperse on a more natural puff of wind. As she turns to face me, she straightens up, clasping her hands in front of her.

"One of my few affinities," she says with a self-deprecating wryness that makes me want to growl in her defense. "Conducting the air—such a useful skill."

She commented before that she didn't think her particular strengths had much purpose. Did that feeling factor into her reasons for leaving her entire realm behind? Did someone back there believe she was unworthy?

If they did, I want to tear into them as much as I do the beast who attacked her.

"We all need the air," I say, groping for the words to convince her that I don't see her talents the same way. "It's the most essential element to life, don't you think?"

Kara's eyebrows arch slightly. "I suppose if I happen to be around when someone's struggling to breathe, that'd be a good thing, but it's not a problem that comes up very often. And usually even in those cases, they need a healer who can work on their lungs, not simply a quick breeze."

She does have a point, but I refuse to concede. "Every talent has its benefits."

"Hmm. We just won't get into the size of those benefits." She motions to the garden around her. "I don't have the true names for most of these plants, but that doesn't stop me from weeding with my hands. I find ways to pitch in."

"You don't need to put yourself to work," I remind her, unable to stop my voice from getting gruff. "You're supposed to be recovering. And you're our guest."

Kara shrugs and offers me a small smile that lights up something inside me that I don't know what to do with. "An unexpected guest whom you have no reason to host other than generosity. I believe in paying back my debts."

Is that really how she thinks we see her—as an expense on our time and resources? I frown, but before I can grumble about her reasoning, she changes the subject with a curious tilt of her head. "What's the main focus of your magic? I haven't seen you working much."

Suddenly the shoe is on the other foot. I have no doubt about the usefulness of my own skills, but they definitely didn't fit anyone's hopes for me in my past life. Much too domestic for a man meant to someday be a lord's cadre-chosen.

Even though Kara has no idea of those expectations, the words always catch in my throat when the topic comes up with anyone other than the two friends who are all I have left of a pack.

"Mainly animals," I say. "I tend to our livestock here— keep them thriving and happy. It extends somewhat into other bodily magic, which is why I'm not too shabby with healing."

I pause, taking in her posture. Is she favoring her side

more than she was yesterday—the side with the cracked ribs? "Speaking of which, I should take another look at you, see if I can speed along the mending more."

Kara stiffens for an instant as if she's going to balk. I'm not giving her a chance to say no. I stride over, and she hops gingerly out of the garden as if she's afraid I'd tramp right onto the plants to get to her if she doesn't move. There's a bird-like grace to the movement that I didn't know I'd admire until I saw it in her.

But then, I haven't spent much time around ravens other than my stints on the front when we were at war rather than in peace. I can't imagine Kara slashing out with beak and talons like those warriors did.

When she comes to a stop next to the garden, it's with a wince. She's definitely in more pain than before. I draw up next to her and hover my hand over her side, not quite touching the fabric of her sleek dress. Even though the enticing scent of her tugs at me much more insistently when we're so close, I narrow all my attention down to the sensations that reach me when I mutter the true name for bone.

Unless my senses are addled, the cracks have opened a little since I last worked my magic on her rather than continuing to heal.

I speak to the bones again, willing the cracked edges to fuse back together, to seal the fractures. The material melds, but not as strongly as I'd prefer. Not for the first time, I wish that my main specialty was the healing arts.

"You've been pushing yourself too hard," I say gruffly, and peer at her with a sudden suspicion. "Have you been shifting?" The transformation from one physical shape to another always puts a strain on the body. It's only a jolt of exertion for someone in good condition, but it can exacerbate injuries.

The guilty pursing of Kara's lips is enough of an answer. "I needed to stretch my wings," she says defensively. "I don't suppose you'd like to go days without releasing your wolf."

No, I wouldn't. But I doubt she just glided around the clearing a few times for her ribs to have been this affected.

I glower down at her as if I can intimidate her into looking after herself. "You need to stay close to our village. Stretch your wings from one building to another, not all the way out into the forest."

She nibbles one of those lips under her teeth in a way that sends a flare of heat through me as I imagine tasting it myself. I yank my lust back under control.

"I know I need to be careful," Kara says, glancing up at me. Is the flush in her cheeks embarrassment at the chiding or is she affected by our nearness too? "I didn't go far enough to bring any trouble down on you."

This time I let out my growl. To my shame, the woman flinches.

I rein in my temper and grasp her shoulder, holding her gaze. "I'm not worried about trouble for *us*. You aren't a problem or an imposition. I'm *glad* that we found you and were able to come to your aid."

"You were that bored before?" she says, with only a faint teasing note in her voice. She doesn't shake off my hand.

"Not bored," I insist. "Fae are meant for more than merely surviving. We haven't had much chance to live since we came here. And protecting someone else's life means more than just about anything else could." I manage to smile. "It also isn't a bad thing to have a little variety in company."

She laughs with a hint of pain that has nothing to do with her injuries—at least not the bodily ones. "My company hasn't been widely sought out. I guess I'm not used to it."

I resist the urge to stroke my hand over her hair in a gesture that might come across as too familiar. But I don't hesitate to say, with all the honesty I can put into the words, "You're welcome to stay here as long as you'd like. We'll be happy to have you. Those of us who don't fit where we were supposed to be have to stick together, don't we?"

I must have said something a little bit right. A flicker of her smile comes back, even if her eyes look sad.

"It's nice to think so," she says, and gestures to a basket at the edge of the garden with a few roots she's dug up. "I should get these to Brice for the dinner. Thank you."

It's only after she's walked away that I realize she never actually agreed with me that she could belong here.

8

Kara

$\mathcal{I}$ linger in the common building after breakfast, not sure what to do with myself. Restlessness winds through my limbs.

I didn't fly out in search of another meeting of the dissidents last night. It seems unlikely that they'd be getting together that often anyway—but I also can't shake the prickle of fear that comes with the memory of my confrontation with them.

Dredging up my past made me feel sick. I'm trying to get as far from the woman who did those things as I can; pretending to *be* her is the last thing I want to do.

And if I try and the hostile fae realize I'm working against them, I may not get any future at all.

It would be a lot simpler to mind my own business and stay out of it, wouldn't it? It didn't sound as if they've made much progress with their plans to disrupt the peace anyway. I can forget whichever of them took a shot at me if they'll leave me alone to live my life too.

I tell myself that, but the thought of the meeting I interrupted still itches at me. I've already seen to the dishes, and I find myself working a cleaning charm on the table and then the floors as well, not that they were particularly dirty. When I'm done, I pause by the pantry, gazing across the eating area with the same vaguely unsettled feeling that I can't seem to shake.

In spite of his height and his vivid coloring, Nyle can be quite stealthy when he wants to be. He slips into the room so abruptly that I startle.

He goes to the kitchen to pick up a goblet. "A little on edge today, raven?"

I rub my mouth awkwardly. "I—not exactly. Just trying to figure out what I can do to contribute around here."

He pours water from the pitcher into the goblet but then simply holds the cup in front of him, turning it in his lean fingers as he arches his eyebrows at me. "Are there not enough entertainments in our makeshift village for your liking?"

I've always found Nyle a little intimidating, but I'm not going to let him heckle me. I wrinkle my nose at him. "That's not what I meant, and I think you know it."

He shrugs with a twitch of his lips that could be a smile or a frown suppressed—I can't tell which. It's hard to decipher any subtle expressions on that deeply scarred face. Talon marks cut across the corner of his mouth, the bridge of his nose, both sides of his jaw.

"What can I know about what goes through a raven's mind?" he says.

His tone is dry rather than accusing, but the question along with those scars brings a question of my own tumbling from my throat. "Are you really okay with me being here? After... I can see you've had at least one bad encounter with the winter fae. I can't imagine you hold many positive feelings toward the Unseelie."

Nyle's eyebrows rise even higher, all the way to the fringe of his bright red hair. "I'm pretty sure you weren't the warrior who dealt the wounds that led to these scars, seeing as I killed that one."

I restrain a wince at the image conjured of a gutted bird. "Obviously not. But lots of fae still have trouble letting go of the decades of animosity—fae who've been less permanently altered by it than you have. It wouldn't be surprising if you held some resentment."

And he's definitely been the least welcoming out of my three hosts, though I'm polite enough not to point that out.

It seems I don't have to. Nyle props himself against the counter and finally takes a sip of his water, watching me over the glass. "If you think I've questioned you because you're Unseelie, you've been unfair. I've been wary of you because you're a stranger. I'd like to believe I wouldn't have treated a random wolf who careened into our midst any differently."

My cheeks flush. "That's reasonable. I just—I wasn't sure."

He shrugs without any sign of real offense taken. "I don't believe in holding petty grudges. And I don't believe in making sweeping assumptions either. Both tend to get people into trouble much more often than out of it. I know how the war between the seasons happened, and it's perfectly understandable. I'm simply glad it's over with now. I prefer the peace. Frankly, I take more issue with what some of my own people have done than with yours, but I don't paint all of Seelie kind with the same brush either."

I suspect he's referring to the events that resulted in Ronan's banishment. But if even Brice is keeping clammed up about that, I can't imagine cool, wary Nyle will fill me in on the details.

"The three of you are definitely proof that you're not all a bunch of bloodthirsty savages," I say, letting my voice take a lilting tone to show I'm teasing. But my gut has clenched.

He talks about leaving behind the past—the war, the damage done to his face—so easily. I don't know if I'll ever be able to look back on the source of the wounds I've taken inside so calmly.

Between the two of us, I'm the more savage one.

Something in Nyle's expression shifts. He steps closer to me, holding my gaze with his gleaming eyes, which make his whole face compelling even with the ridges of scar tissue. His voice comes out as even as before but quieter. "You haven't been treated so well by your own kind either, have you?"

My throat constricts. "It just... worked out that way," I say, because I can't bear to tell him that it's mainly my fault rather than anyone else's.

His approach has sent an uneasy wash of heat over my

body. I find myself groping at the edge of the table as if for balance. "I—I think I've helped as much as I can in here," I add. "I should see if there's anything else to be done in the garden."

Nyle tips his head to me without argument. I can feel him watching me as I flee the common building.

Outside, I'm struck by a similar sense of aimlessness until a faint bleating reaches my ears from beyond the clearing. Ronan mentioned his skill with animals, and I already noticed that the men keep a small, mixed herd nearby. Technically I won't be leaving their home turf.

I stride along the narrow dirt path through the forest, following it over a swift, burbling stream to the edge of a meadow about the same size as the clearing where the men have set up their houses. An open-walled clay structure at the far end provides an overhanging roof that I suppose is for shelter if it rains. In the summer climate, the livestock aren't likely to need a whole barn for warmth the way we have things on the winter side of the border.

None of the animals are taking advantage of the structure's shade right now. A dozen or so goats and as many sheep amble around the meadow, grazing the grass and muttering at one another in their animal way.

I never cared for the pungent smells of the barn back home, but the odors of livestock seem less offensive in the open air where the lush forest scents can mingle with them.

Ronan is perched on a stool not far from the structure, angled away from me. It takes me a moment to make out that he's milking one of the larger goats. It stands there with a dopey expression as he works, whether because it trusts its master or because he's used his magic on it, I can't tell. It's an odd scene, the man built like a hulking warrior going through the careful motions to bring nourishment to the rest of us.

I'm not sure if I should disturb him—or more to the point, the goat. But he must be just finishing, because he gives the doe a gentle smack to her haunches, and she trots off to join her companions.

My mouth is already forming a smile as he turns toward me while picking up the metal jug he aimed the milk into by its handle. He catches sight of me with a flicker of surprise and then a broad smile of his own that warms me from my toes all the way to the top of my head. He starts to stride toward me between the animals.

At the same moment, the largest ram in the bunch decides it's not pleased about my arrival. With a grunt, it springs forward, aiming its horned skull at me.

I'm not in any real danger. The creature only comes up to my elbow, and it isn't moving very fast. But it takes me by surprise, and I let out a yelp as I try to scramble out of the way. One horn smacks against my healing ribs, jolting a hiss of pain out of me.

Then all I hear is a furious roar. An immense black wolf hurtles into the ram and slams it into the ground so hard it bleats in pain. As I stumble backward and trip over a stone, Ronan sinks his fangs into the ram's neck.

"I'm okay!" I babble, the words jolting out of me as I fall on my ass. I scramble back to my feet as hastily as I can. "I'm fine, really. You don't need to hurt it."

I hold out my hand instinctively in a pacifying gesture. A growl reverberates from Ronan's wolfish throat. He hasn't torn open the ram yet, though—it's still shivering beneath him. A tremor runs through his darkly furred frame. Tension radiates off him, and I have the abrupt impression that he's warring with himself. Caught between his calmer awareness and a flare of deep-seated emotion he can't quite master.

Like Grand-da in the middle of one of his episodes. The sense of recognition brings the true name to my tongue before I even think about it. I propel it out in as soothing a tone as I can manage in my startled state. "*Trin-vie-sum-dal.*"

The moment I speak it while I'm focusing on Ronan, impressions of his emotional state sweep through my mind. His heart is racing, every muscle contracted with the urge to rip apart the threat—the threat to me. The sense is reverberating through him that he's an instant away from failing to avert a horrible catastrophe.

"I'm okay," I say again in a softer tone, taking a careful step toward him and the ram. I murmur the true name again, willing his jangling nervous system to settle down, his alarm to subside. "I'm totally all right. It was just a little bump. The ram didn't know who I was. He probably thought he was protecting his ewes. You can let him go."

Gradually, Ronan's body relaxes. He opens his jaw to release the ram and seems to grimace at the sight of the puncture wounds in the creature's neck. With a shake, he's containing his wolf, shifting back into the form of a man, and pressing his hand to the creature's injured flesh with a whispered true name.

It speaks to both his skill and the trust he's already gained with these animals that the ram holds still and lets him seal the toothmarks. As it trots off across the meadow, Ronan exhales shakily and glances around.

He dropped the milk jug in his haste to get to me—it's tipped over on its side, most of the milk pooled and seeping into the ground. His jaw tightens before he straightens up and lets himself meet my eyes.

"I'm sorry," he says. "I—I have trouble reining myself in when I get the impression of someone being threatened."

Somehow I think it's more than that. And if he's always been this way, it's not hard to imagine what kind of "misunderstanding" might have gotten him shunned by his former pack.

My own nerves are buzzing, though, and not with apprehension. He leapt in that fiercely to defend *me* from a threat. He's looking at me now with a feral intensity I've never experienced before, as if he wants to drag me away from anything else that might provoke the slightest pain.

"I can appreciate that," I hear myself saying as if from a distance. "I guess it must also cause problems sometimes."

His lips pull back into something halfway between a scowl and a snarl. "It hasn't come up much. There was—I let someone down. Before. My little sister. And she didn't survive it."

An ache wraps around my heart. Not even a character flaw then but an emotional response triggered by a specific tragedy. My voice comes out hoarse. "I'm sorry."

"Not anywhere near as much as I am." He glances down at his hands. "The thought of it happening again…

But I need to get better control of myself. I'm not helping anyone lashing out at the sheep."

He glances up at me, his gaze as intense as before but with a hint of tenderness. "You did something for me. Guided me out of it."

"My other affinity besides air," I say with a vague motion of my hands. "Nerves—emotions. The Heart decided I should be all about ephemeral things, it seems."

"They're not so ephemeral when you're in the grips of them." He eases closer, watching me as if he thinks I'm going to dart away from him like prey before a predator. "Thank you. I'd have understood if you'd run the other way instead. A raging wolf can be pretty disturbing to witness, especially for someone not accustomed to wolves at all."

Suddenly I've lost my breath. "I wasn't scared," I murmur. "I—I'm honored that it'd matter so much to you to protect me, even if it wasn't totally necessary."

A slow smile spreads across Ronan's mouth, wiping away the concern that had lingered there. He takes another step, close enough now that the heat of his presence tingles over my skin. "Honored, are you? No shying from wolves for this raven?"

"Not from you," I say.

Then he touches my cheek, and my body sways toward him of its own accord. When his lips descend on mine, my entire body lights up with hope and longing.

I kiss him back, letting one arm loop around his neck to pull him even closer, rising up on my toes so I can better meet him. His heat floods me, and in that moment, there's nowhere I'd rather be than caught up in it.

He wants me. He cares about me and he *wants* me.

And Heart help me, I want him too, this damaged but determined wolfish man.

But as he deepens the kiss with a pleased rumble, one chilly thought tickles up from the back of my mind: If he knew who I really was, what I've done, he wouldn't want any of this.

Resolve coils in my chest, heavy but firm.

I've found something good here. I've found a happiness I hadn't expected. And if I'm going to keep it, I need to make sure I'm worthy of it—of this man and his friends who've taken me into their home and under their protection.

Even if that means venturing back out far beyond their protection and into the line of fire.

9

Kara

I t takes three nights of watching before I catch the wolf with the silver-streaked neck leaving the same village where I spotted him before. He slinks off in a different direction from when he headed to the first meeting I interrupted, but I have no doubt that it's the same man, leaving for the same purpose.

The dissidents are gathering again.

I'm not sure if this Seelie is just not very skilled in stealth or if the dissidents have no idea how I found their previous meeting. I follow his scent trail as before, pushing my wings faster when he conjures a hasty carriage out of a juniper sapling and speeds onward that way.

Tonight's meeting must be held farther abroad. I suppose it makes sense that the traitors would want to avoid congregating in the same spot often, or it'd be much easier for someone to notice unusual activity in the area.

The swift movement of the carriage makes the wolfish scent fade faster, but the soft warble of the wind around the craft helps me stay on track. My target can't race ahead *too* quickly since he's sticking to the shelter of treed land wherever he can. The one time we slip across an open field, I let myself hang back and then hurtle forward once he's glided into the span of forest on the other side.

It'll be best if the dissidents *never* realize how I'm tracking them. The Heart only knows how long it'll take before they trust me enough to tell me where they plan to gather next.

Thankfully, the past two nights when I only needed to fly out to this man's village have meant I've given my ribs a decent break. By the time the carriage slows, a dull ache has formed in my chest, but it's much milder than last time. I'll just have to hope I haven't opened the cracks enough for Ronan to notice and chide me about it.

Thoughts of him—of our kiss, of the heated glances and brief touches since then—rise up in my mind as I land on a branch near the glade where several figures are already waiting. A giddy shiver passes through my body. But I don't know what's really happening with him, what he wants from me. Other than the hungry looks and the brushes of his fingers when he passes near me, he hasn't made any further move.

I can't tell whether he's simply waiting out of some sense of honor until he's sure I'm fully healed and not at all dependent on his kindness, or if something else is holding him back. I'm hardly going to throw myself at him. Maybe he's decided anything more than that kiss isn't such a good idea.

The possibility shouldn't bother me so much. I didn't come to the summer realm looking for a roll in the hay with a wolf shifter. But I can't help suspecting that he might be *right* that associating with me is unwise.

I can change that. I can make real amends for the damage I did before. I can be someone who stands up to the villains instead of acting like one.

The wolf I was following joins his fellow traitors. I wait for a few minutes, watching a rat slink out of the shadows and another summer fae enter the glade before I hop down from my branch and shift out of my raven body. The delay will make it harder for them to guess how I've tracked the group to this spot.

The furtive murmurs between the gathered fae fall silent when I step into the glade with my head held high. I fold my arms over the bodice of my dress, a fairly simple one but the most elegant of those I brought with me. I want them to remember that they're dealing with a true-blooded lady, a fae with more claim to our full heritage than any of them, going by the subtler points of their ears where they have much of a point at all.

"You wanted me to prove my commitment," I say, glancing from one to another. "Here I am. I trust you haven't gotten too far into your discussions yet?" Better they think I've only just arrived rather than that I waited a little while observing them.

The Seelie man who took the firmest stance with me before steps a little ahead of the others. I'm not sure if they consider him something of a leader, but *he* obviously thinks of himself as one. He looks me up and down with a hint of a leer in his pale eyes that makes my skin crawl.

He's half a foot taller than me and nearly as broad as Ronan, but nothing about him sparks any attraction in me. The angles of his face look crudely carved, as if he were sculpted by a child who got bored before etching in the finer details, and there's an edge of cruelty to the slant of his wide mouth. The ruff of his dark hair standing up down the center of his head gives a vague impression of a mohawk.

I wonder if it's purposeful or if his hair just grows that way. One of the younger fae in my flock at Hazeleven tried out the style once after some romps beyond the Mists in the human realm, and received such disdain for it that he ended up shaving all his hair off so it could grow back in evenly.

"Kara of Hazeleven," Mohawk says with a sneering curl of his lip. "You think a lot of yourself, don't you?"

"I know who I am and what I'm capable of," I say evenly. "Have I proven myself or not? I'm here. What are we going to do to make some actual progress toward tearing up this treaty?"

The other dissidents shuffle on their feet uneasily, a few of them exchanging caustic mutters between them. The sole raven shifter among them frowns at me but doesn't speak up.

One of the wolfish women bares her teeth in a smile that doesn't look particularly friendly. "We can use her. She knows the arch-lords. She tricked Lady Talia before. She can get to them better than any of us."

I decide not to mention that technically I'm banned

from setting foot anywhere in the arch-lords' domains. The details of my continuing sentence aren't their business. "I'll go as far as I'm able to," I say, which is vague enough to be perfectly true.

Mohawk cocks his head to the side, his gaze turning piercing. "You can't know them very well. That stuffy Unseelie arch-lord wouldn't even have you over a dust-destined human."

I restrain a wince at the sore spot he's prodded. I don't want him to know that any part of me cares about that. "Murk magic addled his head and prevented him from recognizing our connection. It had nothing to do with me."

One of the others lets out a huff. "Just goes to show that the bunch of them aren't thinking straight. We should have kept to our own. Look after our kind and let everyone else do the same."

My gut tightens against the thought of having to agree with that sentiment. Do they really think we were better off when we were at each other's throats, slaughtering each other across the border while the Murk attacked wolves and ravens alike? Even when I was in my darkest moments, I never wanted war over peace.

I just wanted the mate the Heart had intended for me.

The raven motions to me. "How did you manage to trap Lady Talia? She must have been well-guarded. It was quite a feat to pull off."

"Yes!" The wolfish woman runs her hand through her shaggy hair, which is dappled with patches of darker gray and pure white amid the silvery strands. "Let's hear what *your* brilliant plan was. Maybe we can borrow it."

My stomach knots tighter, but I force a smile. "It wasn't actually all that hard... for me. It was a collaboration a lot like you've formed here. I heard that there was a Seelie lord with a particular animosity toward Lady Talia who felt we could end the conflict with the Murk by handing her over. I sought him out and arranged that I would get her into his hands while she was staying on the winter side, where no one would suspect him of making a move."

The raven hums to himself. "And how did you propel her to him, exactly?"

Remembering those moments brings back the queasiness I felt the last time I met with these criminals. I swallow thickly and keep my tone briskly unemotional.

"She'd been healing our curse. I knew she was upset because there were children she hadn't managed to save. I caught her when she was out of the palace with just one guard and convinced her there was another family in need who'd just gone looking for her across the border. I sent her right into the Seelie lord's grasp."

Mohawk snorts. "Is she so simple that she fell for a trick like that?"

I wet my lips. He doesn't believe me.

My stomach lurches harder, but I force myself to say, "I added some magic to the mix. I have a skill with nerves, which can provoke emotion. With that, I made her more panicked and upset than she would have been otherwise. She couldn't think clearly."

And that was the most impressive feat I'd ever pulled off with my ephemeral talents. Not anything I'd brag about in company other than this. My smile feels increasingly stiff as I will back my nausea.

My gambit worked because Lady Talia has a good heart, as human as it might be. She wanted to save all of us, every fae she could. Why wouldn't Corwin have wanted her over me after I'd shown how much venom was in my own heart?

Why would *anyone* want a woman like that? I don't know if I've managed to drain the poison of my resentment all out yet, as much as I've tried. But maybe the new gambit I'm trying here will finally heal the parts of me no healer can tell are broken.

The woman with the patchy hair lets out a triumphant whoop. "Brilliant! That's a skill we could use. Muddling emotions can work to our advantage in so many ways."

"I'm open to suggestion," I say in an arch tone. "But I think we need a more focused plan than that."

"Of course." Mohawk rubs his hands together. "We've started small, but we need to aim big."

"We can't go straight at the most powerful fae around," someone else grumbles.

"Not right now. We'll build up to it." His icy eyes gleam as he looks me over again, with an appreciation that's not at all lustful now but no more comfortable than before. "Now that we have such a helpful ally on our side."

Patchy bobs eagerly on her feet. "It isn't even the arch-lords we need to tackle. Lady Talia has to be removed."

The raven nods. "The peace started with her. Without her, it falls apart."

My pulse skips a beat. I didn't expect them to leap

straight into a conspiracy that huge—one they expect me to take some kind of role in.

I *can't*. The moment they ask me to do anything specific to harm her or confirm a definite scheme of their own, the vow I took that's the other part of my continuing penance will compel me to back away.

"I'd imagine that's true," I say carefully. "But let's take things one step at a time. People have gotten used to the peace. You've been trying to show them it's not worth it, haven't you? We'd need to lay the groundwork before making the biggest move."

Mohawk grins with his fangs showing. "So eager to get to work. I think you'll be a good addition to the crew, Kara of Hazeleven."

I smile back at him, wishing that statement of approval didn't feel so much like a threat.

10

Brice

Kara seems distracted at breakfast. She doesn't speak much, gazing at her plate vaguely between bites as if she's seeing something else altogether. When Ronan makes a few concerned comments, she smiles in a similarly vague way and answers briefly.

"Do you have big plans for today?" I ask in a playful tone, trying to get a better smile out of her.

She blinks at me for a second as if she thinks I might be serious, and then all I get is the same noncommittal expression. "Pretty much the same as usual, I'd imagine."

When we've finished eating, she moves automatically to collect the dishes. She's been handling the cleaning spells since she arrived here, an observation that sends a twinge of discomfort through me.

It must bother Ronan too, because he pushes to his feet, his voice coming out in a growl. "You don't need to do that. You're a guest here, not a servant. Let me take care of them."

"Oh. All right." She ducks her head and slips out of the common building, leaving me wondering if his intervention made things better or worse.

The thought hits me with a sinking sensation in my gut, and I can't shake it once it's snagged in my mind: She's getting ready to leave.

She's been here for a week. Her head's fine, and her ribs are nearly healed. Why wouldn't she want to move on, to continue the travels she originally set out on? Why would she want to stay here with the three of us in our remote village that's barely even a village?

She'd have every reason to go, but the idea unsettles me. I get up, pacing through the room for a minute while Ronan murmurs over the dishes.

Nyle mutters a quick true name to sweep the table clean of crumbs. As he turns toward the door, my voice erupts out of me with an unexpected sense of urgency.

"We should do more."

Nyle pauses and glances back at me.

Ronan turns from where he's just stacked the plates and raises his eyebrows. "More of what?"

I make a hasty gesture with my hands. "We wanted— the whole idea of this place was that we could turn it into some kind of commune for fae who don't have a real place anywhere else. Who've been cast out by or left their packs and flocks for reasons beyond their control. We've been here for years, and we haven't even really started."

Maybe if we had, Kara would *want* to stay. I can tell she wasn't really happy in her old winter domain. She came here searching for something better. But we can't give that to her with what we've set up right now. It's barely a life for even the three of us.

Nyle fixes me with one of those penetrating looks that give me the sense he can see right inside my skull. He always knows how to cut right to the heart of the problem, but thankfully he doesn't tend to be totally brutal about it when he aims his attention at the two of us.

"We can't simply *make* that happen," he says. "I can't imagine getting a good response if we put out some kind of open call, and then we wouldn't be able to pick and choose who we'd want to join us. We have to wait until we hear about someone who might need a place to land, who doesn't sound like an outright criminal or deviant, and then bring them in."

Like we had with Kara. Ronan's jaw twitches as if he's thinking the same thing. He glances around the common building and frowns. "There isn't much here to offer anyone yet, is there?"

"There isn't," I agree.

Nyle shrugs. "It's hard to know what to build if you don't know who you're building it for. We've constructed a home that suits the three of us well enough."

Ronan hums to himself, his expression gone pensive. He moves to the pantry. "We have more cheese from recent milkings than we need for ourselves. I was already planning on going out to a couple of the villages nearby to ask around about raven-haters again. I'll bring a gift along as well—we can recapture at least some of the good favor we've lost."

Nyle watches him with a nod. "It'll just take time." He glances at me and arches his eyebrows. "Are you feeling impatient for more company, little brother? Missing the hustle and bustle of home?"

I'm not actually his brother, but the three of us are close enough that we might as well be family. I grimace at his teasing tone. "Not like that. I just..." I let my voice drop, unsure how keen Kara's hearing is. "Having someone else around with different ideas and experiences has reminded me how enjoyable that can be. And that I'd like to continue enjoying that."

Nyle's eyebrows shoot a little higher, which tells me he doesn't believe I'm only interested in Kara for conversation. Well, he can think whatever he wants. I'm not ashamed of finding her attractive.

"I suppose you'd better make a convincing case to her then, until we've made this spot more of an ideal destination," he says, and cracks his knuckles. "I'm going to have another prowl through the territories around us for signs of her attacker. He may have lain low for a while hoping we'd come off our guard, but that doesn't mean he won't make another attempt."

As my friends head out, a hollow sensation fills my chest. I've been making demands about what we need to accomplish here, but how much have *I* contributed to turning this place into more of a home?

I created the foundations of the buildings, but that was done ages ago. My work with the soil helps keep the garden producing well, I suppose. Otherwise, I haven't been much more use here than I was back home.

I step out into the clearing and find myself meandering over to Kara's house. With a prick of my ears, I determine she isn't inside. I pick up soft sounds of movement from the other side of the common building—she must be puttering around in the herb garden there.

The sight of the structure I made for her fills me with even more dissatisfaction. It's a crude shape barely worthy of being called a house, with none of the careful details I brought to the older buildings. I didn't have much time when I first raised it, but I have since then. I can make it more comfortable for her—more worthy of her.

With a few murmurs under my breath, the dense, steady energy of the earth resonates through my body. I press my hands to the side of the building and will the hard-packed dirt to adjust its form. A ledge at the base of the window, level enough that she could set things on it. A tighter fit for the door so that her privacy is more assured. I will the roof to lift into an elegant arch to give the interior both an airier feel and a more pleasant appearance.

It isn't much, but sometimes the little details can make all the difference when it comes to comfort.

When I've finished, I step back to consider the structure, wondering if there's anything else I should add. My mind slips back to the sweeping castle back at Saplight, the pearly walls and pale furniture I grew up around.

The riches I was surrounded by never really felt like home. They never really felt as though they were *mine*. But there were parts of it I gravitated to. The hearth-room with its massive fireplace and thick rugs. The gymnasium my older sister, the true-blooded child, set up at the back full of bars and ropes for physical training, that I'd sneak into when I was sure no one needed it more urgently.

And outside the castle, what was there that made the village an actual community and not just a collection of houses? The revels my mother liked to host every week around the bonfire pit? The beachy area a few of my former pack-kin created at the edge of the lake?

I'm so lost in thought I don't hear Kara approaching until she's just a few paces away. She stops at the turn of my head and looks over her refined house.

"You didn't need to do any of that," she says.

"You don't need to clean or help with the gardens or anything else," I point out automatically. "But it matters to you all the same."

She makes a dismissive sound. "You're already doing plenty for me just by letting me stay here and helping me heal."

"I'd like to think that's the bare minimum." I pause, weighing my words, not liking to get too serious but feeling I need to say *something* meaningful if she's going to understand just how welcome she is here. "It's sounded like you've been adrift for a while. Maybe even when you were still in your original domain. I know what that feels like—and I think everyone deserves to have somewhere they really feel at home."

Something shifts in Kara's face, a flicker of longing and a stiffening of hesitation. She wets her lips, her gaze darting away from me and then back again. "Is that what *you'd* really want? For me to make this place my home?"

I can almost taste the hope she's trying to restrain that bleeds into her voice all the same. It makes me want to wrap my arms around her and hug her tight, but I have no idea how a gesture that forward would be received.

So I simply smile and say, "I would. I think all three of us would. We always meant to expand this into a real village when we encountered like-minded fae who didn't really have a place elsewhere."

But just because she didn't feel at home back in the winter realm doesn't mean there's nothing there she misses. If I have fond memories of my former domain, she must too. I should be focusing on what *she'd* want to see here to make this place more of a community she could belong to, not what I'd like.

Before she has to respond to my previous remarks, I sweep my arm to indicate both her house and the open stretch of clearing beyond it. "Even if you don't decide to stay much longer, we'd still like to make this a spot where Unseelie can fit in just as well as Seelie like us. What did you like the most back in the domain where you grew up? Things you've had to go without since you left?"

Kara's eyes go as distant as they were during breakfast, but I don't mind when I know she's focused on giving me a definite answer. She tips her head to one side, the sunlight catching on the graceful planes of her pretty face.

To look at her, you wouldn't think she'd be out of place among typical cool and elegant winter face. She's lovely to behold, she's clearly true-blooded, and I can't find any fault in her manners.

But her constant need to make herself useful, to pay us back for our hospitality, speaks of an open heart that I didn't think most of the ravens appreciated all that much. The ones I've met kept their feelings close and their dealings cautious. She cares and isn't afraid to show it.

And every time I can bring a smile to her face, it feels like a victory.

"Because we were near the fringes, we got a lot of snow," she says. "If it wasn't too bad a storm, there were a couple of artists in my flock who'd put on a show, lighting up the flakes with different colors and moving them around with their magic, almost like a painting turned into a puppet show. It was pretty fantastic to see." One corner of her mouth ticks upward. "But I don't imagine I'll be getting any snow around here."

I laugh. "No, that's one thing the summer realm is entirely deficient in. Is there anything else?"

"I guess a lot of the parts I appreciated are things like that. On still days, we had a courtyard we'd sometimes gather in where the stones that lined it radiated heat, and we could soak in the sun and the contrast between the cool breeze and the wafts of warmth... Here, everything is warm."

"If not hot," I say lightly, but my mind is suddenly spinning through the possibilities. Of course she'd miss the sensation of true coolness when that's the atmosphere she's most used to. I can't imagine going without the summer warmth for ages.

Inspiration sparks, rippling through my thoughts. I'm so pleased with my brainstorm that I can't stop myself from grinning at her.

"I know just what you need—and any other ravens who stop by will be thankful for it too. You're familiar with saunas, where the point is to bask in heat? I can raise a building that does the opposite. You could slip inside and soak in a chill to escape from our relentless sun for a little while."

Kara blinks in surprise. "You could make something like that?"

"I'm sure of it. I'd use the same principles as we put toward the cold box in the pantry, just magnified in size. I'm no slouch when it comes to water, you know—it works in harmony with earth. Ice is just hardened water. And even in the summer realm, if you dig down deep enough…"

I speak the true name for earth and water and then reach my awareness down into the ground beneath my feet. Onward and onward to where the sun's heat no longer reaches, to where the dark depths are full of cool moisture.

Yes. Perfect. Forming the syllables on my tongue again, I tug at the materials I can sense. I draw them up through the ground and shape them to my will as they come.

Each block needs to be larger than the basic bricks I'd typically create to hold enough water inside them to provide the cooling effect. I'd want the building to be the size of a sauna, room for at least a few people to lounge inside, in case we ever have more than one raven staying here.

Who knows—maybe my friends and I will even develop an appreciation for the cold.

My first haul is enough to conjure three earthen blocks. Glancing around, I wave them toward a clear span of earth several paces from Kara's house. I can always move the structure later. I set them in the beginnings of a foundation, close my eyes, and reach back downward, aiming to grab more this time.

My next attempt produces five blocks and a breathless tremor through my chest. It definitely takes more effort hauling the earth from that far down than working with what's close to the surface. But as I set them in place, creating one corner of the building's base, Kara kneels next to them.

She rests her hands on the hardened surface and lets out a gasp of pure delight at the chill I know must be seeping from them. "Wow. That's amazing. Won't they... melt, or whatever?"

I walk over to join her, swiping at the sweat that's formed on my brow. "I'll need to periodically firm up the ice, but the earth is packed tightly enough that it'll insulate it well. It might be a little while before I can have the whole building constructed, but you get the general idea. What do you think?"

"It'll be wonderful." She stands up and turns toward me, her eyes so wide and shining that my heart flips over. Her mouth opens and closes as if she isn't sure what to say. Then she rests her fingers on my forearm, just below my elbow.

Ronan mentioned to us that Kara had a skill with nerves—that she was able to calm him out of his reflexive rage the other day. Even so, I'm not prepared for the rush of sensation that sings through my awareness, stirring up my emotions.

Joy. It's pure joy she's setting alight in me—sharing

with me, to show me how happy my offering has made her.

When I catch her eyes, she's smiling hesitantly but hopefully. I beam right back at her, aglow with plenty of happiness of my own—and not a small amount of affection.

Maybe I could have drawn her into my arms right then. Maybe she'd have welcomed even more than that. But my gaze drops to her mouth, to the petal-soft curve of her lips, and the next thing I know she's easing back with a slight blush coloring her cheeks.

"Thank you," she says. "Really. I don't know how to thank you enough."

"You already have," I say, but my stomach twists with the realization that *she* doesn't believe that, no matter what I tell her.

And I have no idea how to convince her that she's an enhancement to our lives, not a burden.

11

Kara

*N*erves are supposed to be my speciality, but I appear to have lost control over my own. They've been on edge ever since I snuck back into my house late last night after the meeting of the dissidents. Any time one of my hosts makes a swift movement or a louder than usual sound, I have to stop myself from jumping.

If I can't simmer down, they're going to realize that something's wrong.

It's hard not to feel even more guilty than I already did as I watch Brice set a few more blocks on the growing walls of the cold-sauna he's making for me. Well, maybe not entirely for me, since he suggested other Unseelie arrivals might use it at some point, but I know he was mostly trying to make me feel at home.

The way his face lit up when I showed him how much I appreciated the gesture... My heart thumps faster just remembering it.

How am I supposed to keep a cool head when I have three men who are so appealing constantly around me?

How can I believe I'm worthy of the efforts they're going to on my behalf when there's so much I'm hiding from them?

Over dinner, Ronan announces that we should have a bonfire. I'm not sure if Brice filled him in on our conversation about communal activities or if he simply feels he needs to be an even more active host, but he hustles around the sort-of village grabbing supplies, barking orders, and being a general terror until Nyle yanks me toward the forest.

"We can gather some wood," he says in his even voice. "From the sounds of it, we're going to need a stack as tall as he is."

The remark brings a giggle to my throat, the first real laugh I've managed today. As I tramp between the trees in the dimming twilight after Nyle's muscular form, my spirits lighten just a little.

Nyle doesn't try to spoil me. Nyle recognizes that I'm a stranger, someone he shouldn't necessarily trust out of hand. I think I've earned enough trust that he's not actively wary of me anymore, but I doubt he's going to act in any way that'll tie my gut up in guilty knots.

I'm bending to snatch up sticks at random, focusing on the thicker ones that have fallen to the ground. Nyle glances over and tuts his tongue at me. "Those will work for kindling, but we can do better for the main event. Haven't you ever made a fire before?"

I glower at him. "Of course. But wood is wood. At least, we didn't worry much about it back... back home, other than avoiding one type that gave off more smoke than anyone liked."

"Hmm. Maybe we care more about our fires because we summer fae celebrate the heat more." He wields one stick as thick as my wrist, the back smooth and gray. "Ashvein. Burns bright and clear, with shifting colors that make it very enjoyable to watch." He holds up another, this one thinner with gnarled bits and rough bark that's nearly black. "Sickleshade. Works well in combination with ashvein. Its flames and those around them shoot up higher but give off few sparks."

I look down at the bundle in my arms and realize I've only gotten one of the smooth type and none of the other. "Well, thank you for the lesson in summer-realm trees. I'll try to select better from here on."

"It's all right. I should have known not to expect good taste in fire from a raven."

My gaze flicks to him, but he's smiling his thin, reserved smile, so I'm pretty sure he's only teasing. It's not always easy to tell with him.

After that, I make a point of only picking up the branches I spot that fit one of the examples he showed me. Nyle loads up the cart he's brought with us twice as fast. I don't hear him speaking any magic-laced words, but I wouldn't be surprised if he knows the true name for one or both trees and is using it to find their leavings faster.

For a while, there's just the crunching of our

footsteps over the floor and the rustling of the leaves overhead. A pleasantly cool breeze winds through the summery heat. But the silence starts to gnaw at me. My mind drifts back to my conversation with Brice this morning.

"Do you miss much about your old home?" I venture.

Nyle's head jerks toward me so fast I'd think I'd offended him, but when I look over to check his expression, it's as unfazed as ever behind the ridges of his scars.

"Not particularly," he says without any sign of emotion. "I wasn't all that appreciated by the rest of the pack. The only kin I'd have wanted to keep are the two here with me."

I guess it wasn't much of a sacrifice for him to leave with Ronan, then. But an unexpected prickle of frustration runs through my chest. "They should have appreciated you. You obviously fought hard for them."

I can understand why my flock wasn't too fond of me in the last several years, but his pack didn't have that excuse.

Nyle lets out a sharp chuckle. "Oh, I'd imagine they were quite happy with me when I was out fighting on the front. It was less fun for them to be reminded of those struggles every time they looked at my face once I got back."

He manages to stop all but a tiny hint of pain from creeping into his voice. My stomach ends up knotting after all.

He knows what it's like to be shunned by the community that was supposed to be his—and he didn't deserve the shunning, not like I did. He should have been celebrated for the sacrifice he made.

But all the same, he's handled his ill fortune better than I have. He found friends he could trust, and he built something new with them. All I've been able to do is intrude on the start of the new life they were already making for themselves.

"I'm sorry," I say.

Nyle shrugs and tosses his load into the cart. "It's no great tragedy. The way I am means I get to observe people react as they really are upfront rather than waiting to see when their facades will crack. No need to waste time on those who'd consider me unworthy of theirs."

I lug my armful over to the cart and drop it in, unsure of what to say. But when Nyle turns away from me, I find myself grasping his arm. I tug him around to face me and peer up at him, tracing the lines of his scars and the features amid them with my eyes.

Nyle gazes back at me, his face still but his body tensing slightly. Does he expect *me* to find him unworthy?

If anything, the confrontation I've forced is affecting me more than I was ready for—in the opposite direction. Our closeness sends a flush over my skin.

I want to reach inside him and pull out all the thoughts and emotions he's holding so closely guarded behind those piercing eyes. And I find him striking to look upon regardless of the scars. Really, those jagged lines transform him into something more than most fae are.

The boldness rises up in me to lift my hand and trace my fingers carefully over his cheek. My voice comes out breathy. "All I see is how fiercely you'll fight to protect what matters to you. Anyone who thinks the marks of that devotion make you anything other than twice as handsome isn't worth considering."

Nyle exhales in a rush and catches my wrist. His gaze sears into mine. "What are you doing, little raven?"

"I—"

I'm not really sure. I know what I want, but I wanted Ronan the other day. I still want him, and I wanted Brice this morning, and I hardly believe I deserve any of them.

In my hesitation, Nyle releases me and steps away. He glances down at the cart, his usual calm settling over him again. "I think we have enough firewood to satisfy Ronan now. Let's get back to him before he sets the whole clearing up in flames with impatience."

I follow him through the woods, unable to find the right words to rebuild the bridge I thought I'd formed between us. Or else unable to convince myself that I should try.

The other men meet us at a fire pit I hadn't even realized existed, cleared of the long, flat stones that lay on top of it before which now form a circle of seats around it. Ronan and Brice move to grab some of the sticks and heap them on the bare earth within its ring of smaller stones. But naturally it's Nyle of the fiery hair who snaps his fingers, mutters a true name, and sends flames licking over the wood.

Brice has brought a summer type of mushroom I've never tried before, which we poke with longer sticks and hold over the fire to roast before digging into the flesh that's a mix of savory and sweet. As I pause after my second, I find myself studying our arrangement around the fire.

The three men are sitting within a foot of each other on one of the stone benches. I've ended up apart from them, off to the side. Ronan glances over at me, and his lips start to curl with a smile, but then his gaze flicks to Brice, whose attention has just focused on me too. Ronan tugs his eyes back to the fire without finishing his smile.

Suddenly I understand why he's held back since our kiss in the pasture. He does want me, but he's worried his friends do too. They matter enough to each other that the other two voluntarily banished themselves to stick with him. Of course he wouldn't want to do anything that might threaten their bond of friendship.

And he might not be wrong. I don't think I imagined the heat in Nyle's gaze tonight. I could taste the hunger flavoring Brice's eagerness to cater to me this morning. It's resonating through me, fanning my own desires.

As I watch the firelight dance over their very different but equally stunning faces, a strange emotion unfurls inside my chest. Why am I worrying about whether I'm worthy of any of them? I don't expect them to make me their mate or offer any commitments. I wouldn't be *harming* them by satisfying the desires that've been growing inside all of us.

It could be a little sweetness we'd share, something to make my stay here about more than them going out of their way to look after a wounded traveler.

And it doesn't have to divide them either. If Lady Talia can have *five* mates, three of them now arch-lords and all of them fully devoted to her, then why shouldn't I be able to indulge in the pleasures of three for just one night or a few?

If they'd be willing. If none of them feel there's no point unless I'm focused solely on them alone. But there's no way to find that out unless I try, is there?

I came out here to figure out what I want out of the new life I need to build, and right now, what I want is *them*.

I hesitate for a second, and then I push to my feet. All three men fix their gazes on me as I walk over, the wafting warmth of the fire catching in the folds of my dress and the waves of my hair.

I stop in front of the three of them, knowing the flames will be lighting me up from behind. I could bring out my wings and make myself even more of a visual spectacle, but I balk at the idea of reminding them of our differences right now.

The trouble is, I don't really know how to do this. I've never seduced a man before. My feminine wiles, such as they are, weren't enough to win my actual soul-twined mate over. I had a few brief dalliances with men of the flock in my earlier youth, just to get my bearings and enjoy ourselves, but I'm hardly an expert of the carnal arts.

"Kara?" Ronan says in a questioning growl, his gaze never leaving me.

I wet my lips. "I thought maybe we could start a different sort of fire, all four of us. If that's something you'd want too. I like all of you. I want all of you. I don't see why… there'd be any need to choose or leave anyone out, if we all feel the same way…"

A heat wraps around me that has nothing to do with

the fire at my back. It's emanating from the men in front of me.

Ronan stands first, looming over me. He cups my jaw with his massive hand and holds my gaze. His voice comes out ragged but firm. "You don't owe us this. We'd never have asked—"

"I know," I break in before he needs to go on. "I promise you it's got nothing to do with any sense of obligation. I—I haven't met many men I was interested in enjoying a night with." My gaze darts from him to his friends still seated on either side of him. "To meet three at the same time... I'm a very lucky woman. If *I'm* not asking too much."

Brice gets up with an audible swallow. His hand reaches toward me as if drawn by a magnetic force. He trails his fingers down the silky sleeve of my dress to my bare elbow. "Just for tonight?"

My cheeks flush. "I suppose it wouldn't have to be. We could see how it goes? I'm not expecting more than that."

Is he asking because *he'd* want more, or because he wants to make sure I won't demand it? I can't tell.

A rumble forms in Ronan's throat. "We've shared a few times before," he says slowly, whether because he's trying to convince himself or the others, I don't know either. "I don't see why we couldn't again."

He catches Brice's eyes and receives a shy smile in return, then looks toward Nyle.

The scarred man eases himself onto his feet, glancing from his friend to me. As usual, I can't read his expression at all, but his gaze feels as scorching as it did in the woods just an hour ago.

"And how do you see this going, little raven?" he asks in a low voice.

My cheeks flare hotter. "I don't know. *I've* never done anything like this before. But… maybe the three of you have some ideas?"

That's all the prompting Ronan needs to grasp my waist and pull me to him. His mouth descends on mine, branding my lips with a passion that radiates all through my body and has my desire soaking the fabric between my legs.

An encouraging whimper works from my throat. I grip the front of his shirt as if holding on for dear life amid the rush of sensation.

Another hand, so gentle I know it must be Brice's, strokes up and down my back. He caresses his fingers over my ass and then back up to my shoulder. There, he hooks them around the neckline of my dress and pulls it to the side so he can claim that shoulder with a searing kiss of his own.

My heart is already thumping twice as fast. It leaps to an even giddier rhythm when another set of deft fingers start to undo the clasps on the back of my dress. Nyle leans close enough for his breath to tickle through my hair and nuzzles the side of my head.

I feel as if I could melt into all of them. They really are setting me on fire in the best possible way from every side.

When Ronan releases my lips with a growl, it's only to drop his mouth to brand my neck next. I turn my head to give him better access, and my mouth collides with Nyle's.

The normally detached man grips my hair and melds my lips with his hard enough that the edges of his teeth nick my skin, but the sparks of pain only make the pleasure of it sear hotter.

I've never been with three men at the same time before —and I've never been with any summer fae at all. The blaze of their passion sets my memories of my Unseelie lovers in pale relief, awkwardly chill moments of supposed intimacy.

I've never felt as close to anyone as I do to these three now.

I kiss Nyle back with all I have in me, swaying back against Brice's hand when he dips it inside my open dress and runs it down my spine. As Ronan peels the bodice of my dress downward, I turn my head again, seeking out my third lover's mouth.

Brice is there to meet me, his kiss softer but just as enthusiastic as his friends'. His hand slips around to fondle one of the breasts Ronan just bared. The sweep of his thumb draws my nipple to a sudden peak and a gasp from my throat, followed by a breathless moan when the other man laps his tongue over my other breast.

There's so much bliss, my head spins with it. I can barely focus on what I'm doing, where I want this to go, but I hold on to enough conviction to fumble with the collars of the men's tunics, one and then another. If I'm going to be stripped naked, I want to see them too. I want all the sculpted muscle I've admired on full display.

Nyle obliges first, revealing a brawny expanse of pale skin broken by just a few smaller scars and dozens of true name marks. He tosses his shirt aside and then gets to work dragging my dress the rest of the way down my thighs. He catches my undergarments too, and everything pools around my feet in a pile of fabric.

I'm utterly nude but encased in the warmth of these men's bodies. Ronan pulls back to rake his gaze over me and lets out a feral groan. He rips his own shirt off, and his mouth stretches into a grin I can only describe as wolfish when I tease my fingertips over all that solid muscle, stretching across shoulders even broader and a height even taller than his friend's.

A groan reverberates out of him, and then he's kissing me again. I lose myself for a minute in his scorching mouth and the strokes of three pairs of hands over my skin.

Nyle stays crouched by my legs, nibbling a giddy path down my thigh to my knee while he caresses my calf. Brice continues working over my breast with waves of delight, his breath spilling over my shoulder.

My hand catches on his shirt too. When Ronan lets me go, I look toward the slimmer man, and he smiles much more slyly than before. He lets me help him tug off his tunic and then steps closer so I can trace my fingers over the lean panes of muscles beneath his tan skin and his own assortment of true names.

"You're a delicacy," he murmurs, paying back my caresses with more of his own. "So lovely."

Another blush burns my cheeks. I want to return the compliment somehow, but then Ronan sweeps me right off my feet into his bulging arms.

"We can find a better spot than this," he grumbles, and carries me past the stone benches to a strip of thick, satiny grass several paces from the fire.

It doesn't matter that we've left the flames behind. We've generated plenty of our own between our bodies— and none as hot as when Ronan lays me on the cushion of grass and lowers his head between my legs.

His mouth closes over my sex. His tongue swipes over my most sensitive parts from clit to slit, and a headier moan reverberates out of me. My fingers clutch at his bristly hair, my hips rocking in time with the movements of his mouth. Every swivel of his tongue and graze of his teeth sends another needy noise bursting from my lips.

I've never acted so wanton. Never behaved in such an openly undignified way. But I can't summon a single particle of me that cares.

There's nothing shameful about this wildness. I know what true shame is.

Nyle and Brice have knelt on either side of me. As Brice leans in to claim another kiss and drink my lustful noises from my mouth, Nyle looks at Ronan. The other man has raised his head to let his breath spill over my nether regions, which are aching for more.

"How does she taste, brother?" Nyle asks raggedly, as if he's imagining himself in Ronan's place.

"Like duskapple wine," Ronan rumbles, and dives back in for more.

Pleasure spikes through my belly. I arch into his mouth with a strained whimper. Every nerve is thrumming, every inch of me throbbing for more, but I'm not quite there.

If Ronan had brought his fingers to bear, that might have tipped me over the edge. But he seems to want more for me—and for his friends—than that. He suckles me hard one last time and then eases back with a flick of his tongue over his glistening lips as if I really am a delicacy he's savoring the lingering flavor of.

His gaze rises to Brice, who's just raised his own head. "Take her the rest of the way there, my friend? She deserves a gentle start, and I don't think I can give her that."

I would protest, but Brice loosens his trousers without hesitation, and the sight of his cock, long and thrillingly erect, jolts the words from my throat. He catches my eyes, and when I reach for him, he rewards me with the most brilliant of his smiles. His own dark eyes smoldering, he moves over me like a wolf on the prowl.

I spread my legs instinctively, raising my knees. The men around me let out a collective groan. Brice grips my hips and slides into me with one thrust that's determined in its gentleness.

He fills me so fully that I can't restrain another moan. This is what I needed. I clutch at his shoulder, bucking upward to urge him on.

A growl slips from his lips, and he plunges into me harder, faster. His claws must poke from his fingertips, because thrillingly sharp tips graze my thighs where he's pulling me close against him.

"So good," I mumble. "So close."

"I'll take you there, beautiful one," he promises. The speed of his thrusts picks up even more. His hips crash into mine, the base of his cock rubbing my clit, and I shatter apart in a wave of bliss.

Brice sucks in a breath as I clench around him. After a

few more erratic thrusts, he stiffens, spilling himself inside me.

I know before he even slides out of me that we're not done yet, but Nyle doesn't waste any time. He looms over me, his bright eyes shining like copper in the firelight, and flips me onto my hands and knees in one smooth movement.

I've barely had time to squeak in surprise before he's plunging into my slick channel from behind, filling me with a shaft thicker than Brice's. The heady stretch tells me it's a good thing his friend warmed me up.

My head droops downward, my breath coming in pants as I push back against Nyle's forceful thrusts. He pounds into me with none of his friend's initial tenderness, but I can feel the hunger in the grip of his fingers against my waist, in the nearly frantic breaths that rush against my back where he's bowed over me.

The surge of ecstasy is swelling even faster than before. Ronan kneels by my head to lift it with a yank of my hair and crushes his mouth against mine. At the hint of my tart flavor on his lips, a different sort of longing tingles through me.

I drop my head and manage to reach for his trousers. With a growl of understanding, he jerks them down to free his cock. I flick my tongue over its bulbous head, and his breath shudders.

"Oh, my treasure," he mutters. "If it pleases you."

It does, so very much that I close my lips right around him. With a grunt, he grips my hair even tighter and rocks into my mouth.

I suck and swirl my tongue and drink in the musky

flavor of him, caught between him and Nyle in a whirlwind of pleasure. Nyle hisses and digs his unclawed fingers into my hip. The sign of his fracturing control sends me spiraling into my own release.

I cry out around Ronan's cock, my channel clamping around Nyle's shaft. Nyle lets out a choked sound, flooding me with heat.

In the midst of the flood of ecstasy, I tighten my lips around Ronan again. He thrusts into my mouth with a groan and then rips himself away to spill his seed into the grass.

I would have swallowed it, but it's too late to argue about the matter. I let out a shaky sigh, and the massive man catches me up. He spins me onto my back again, cradling me against his immense form.

I offer him a slightly delirious smile, then aim the same at Brice, who crouches by my head, and Nyle, who's sprawled out near my legs.

"I think that was immensely satisfying for all of us," Ronan remarks in a low rumble that sends a fresh quiver of delight through my nerves.

I hum and bury my face in the crook of his neck. "Indeed."

The chuckles that carry around me hold nothing but warmth. I want to drift in this passionate peace forever... but if one night is all I get, then I'll have to make sure it's enough.

12

Nyle

There's nothing wrong with my bed. I shaped the thickly woven mattress and the bronze frame it lies upon to my liking when we first set up our new home here, and it's as comfortable as it ever was.

The problem is that *I'm* uncomfortable in myself. When I close my eyes, images of Kara's lithe body and her pretty face flushed with pleasure flood my mind. Every brush of the bedcovers over my body when I adjust my position brings back the feel of her soft skin against mine. The thrilling slick heat of her cunt welcoming my cock.

A heady shiver races through me, my member rising to half-mast as if urging me to have another go. But tonight's interlude has already overwhelmed so much of my internal state that it unnerves me.

It's been a few years since I was last with a woman—

but I had longer dry spells than that before. I've always been careful in my partners and never found any I wanted to commit to for very long.

But I wasn't so careful with Kara, was I? She tumbled right into our lives almost literally, and we still don't really know why. But that didn't stop any of us from taking her up on her offer tonight.

I stifle a groan of frustration, roll onto my side, and come to the conclusion that I'm not getting any sleep for at least a little while longer, even if it's now well past midnight. Gritting my teeth, I push out from under the covers and shift into my wolf form before I've even shouldered past the door.

Stars glint in the sky overhead, but I can taste a hint of rain on the wind. Not tonight but tomorrow we should have a decent fall. We're in the midlands, not especially close to the Heart but a good distance from the fringelands too, and bad weather mostly comes overnight. Although I can't say a good run in a light shower is necessarily unpleasant.

I enter the woods at a trot that quickly expands into a lope and then a full-out run. Stretching my muscles until they tingle with a faint burn of strain, I race between the trees, dodging protruding roots and jutting shrubs. My world narrows down to the pounding of my feet against the earth and the thump of my pulse behind my ears.

The burn brings a tart sort of clarity to my thoughts. I *haven't* been careful. I tried to be, studying our wintery visitor and asking her questions while my friends have prowled around her protectively, but I haven't really pushed her. Ronan would have had my head if I'd badgered her too much.

I know she's hiding things. It's obvious in the odd hesitations that pop up here and there when there's no reason I can see for her to balk. In the way she speaks sometimes, as if she's skirting around subjects she doesn't even want to hint at.

I have no idea *what* the rest of her story is. It might not be anything that should trouble us. We haven't exactly been totally forthright about what brought us to this remote spot on our own either.

But I can't help thinking I should have waited until I knew more before getting so very concretely entwined with her.

And how will Ronan and Brice react now if something goes sideways with our raven guest? They were already increasingly smitten with her, and acting on those feelings has likely only intensified them.

I know that's happened with my own interest in her. The flickers of attraction I'd felt and attempted to smother have flared and spread into a steady warmth of fondness that's tickling through my veins even now.

I push myself faster, ignoring the bite of a sharp twig against the pad of one of my paws. The wind ripples over my fur, but it isn't enough to wash away my uneasiness.

Before, I couldn't do enough. I didn't intervene fast enough. I didn't recognize the problem in time to help Ronan come up with a proper plan rather than charging in full of rage. Maybe there wasn't anything I *could* have done, but the failure gnaws at me regardless.

He wouldn't even let me speak up on his behalf. It's

possible our pack would have dismissed my claims no matter how baldly I stated them, but I don't know that.

He wanted to keep memories untarnished, though. And I can't help suspecting that he believed he deserved his banishment for his own failure. That in a way, what they'd accused him of was true, even if not in the way they thought it was.

A growl at the memory seeps from my wolfish lips. I hurtle on even faster—too fast.

My shoulder glances off a tree trunk I didn't give quite enough berth. I stumble sideways, my pace thrown off. It isn't a serious blow, but an ache radiates through my front leg as I steady myself.

I shake my body with a huff and look around, scenting the air. I've come a few miles from the village. A different sort of discomfort grips me.

I don't like leaving our home while the others are sleeping. After my time on the front, the slightest disturbance or shift in scent will wake me. My friends aren't quite as alert.

No threat has come for us in the years we've been living in this spot, but that doesn't mean it never will. Especially when we can't be totally sure what our unexpected guest might bring with her, purposefully or otherwise.

Setting a brisk but not reckless pace, I head back toward the village—if you can really call it that. Brice's comments about bringing in more outcasts like us rise up from the back of my mind.

We did talk about that goal when we first set out and put down roots here. It was always him and Ronan who were more eager about the idea of establishing a larger community, though. What I said to Kara this evening was true—my only real community even back in Saplight was the two men I'm living with here.

But I can't deny that her presence has brightened our existence in certain ways. Added a splash of color and excitement that hadn't been there before. Not all of that excitement is good, since the idea of her attacker still lurking out there rankles me, but it's a change of pace all the same. I can't claim that's entirely a bad thing either.

I'll have to keep my ear to the ground for rumors of other vagabonds. It would make my friends happier, at the very least. And maybe Ronan's jolts of aggression would fade away if he had more opportunity to interact with people other than us, people he could trust and tend to.

I've formed that resolve with a mild sense of satisfaction when a whiff of odor that doesn't belong in our territory at all prickles in my nose. I freeze, taking a deeper breath.

There's no mistaking it. A *rat* has crept through this stretch of forest recently.

I bare my fangs automatically. The rodent tried to cover its tracks, the scent faint even though the wisps of it I do catch taste fresh, but it wasn't taking enough care to avoid my keen senses.

My first urge is to lunge forward, charging toward wherever the vermin might be. I stiffen my legs and close my eyes for a second.

The rats aren't automatically our enemies anymore. For thousands of years, they brought nothing but pranks and spite, but they're part of the new peace our arch-lords have formed as much as wolves and ravens are. Three of the Murk sit on thrones by the Heart alongside their Seelie and Unseelie counterparts. One of them shares a mate with two of those counterparts.

They have been hard on us, but we were hard on them too. And from what I've heard, they had a psychotic king egging them on. Now he's dead, killed by the same woman who called so adamantly for peace, and the rats who've come to the Mists asking for mercy have been given that.

It just takes time for old habits to dwindle. I only fought the ravens for a few decades—and we were only at war because of the curse the Murk king inflicted on us. I've been taught to loathe the rats for the entire two and a half centuries I've been alive, by pack-kin who've hated them their entire lives as well. It was rat shifters whose tricks killed my parents and left me adrift within that pack as a child.

But if I can give a chance to a raven after the scars I've been dealt by their kind, then I can hold myself back from assuming the worst of a rat as well.

I trot forward, following the trail but at a warier pace than my first inclination. My ears stay pricked, my lips parted to drink in every trace of that scent.

It leads me toward the clearing where we've made our home, but before it comes to the edge of the woods, it veers to the right. I slow even more, picking up the murmur of hushed voices, too distant for me to make out the words yet. I set my paws gingerly as I stalk around the clearing.

The scent trail only moves into the clearing when I'm right across from the new house Brice constructed for

Kara. I pause, eyeing the building and then inhaling more of the air.

The rat's trail leads that way, but a slightly fresher scent weaves off in the opposite direction, deeper into the woods. The direction the voices are coming from. And I catch a tendril of the raven woman's coolly sweet scent too, drifting along the same course.

My stomach tightens. I don't let my thoughts spiral into paranoia, but that requires clamping down on my mind as I prowl toward the voices.

I will not assume. I will not speculate. I will see what there is to see and hear what there is to hear, and decide what to believe based on the actual evidence.

The words become clear before I can see the speakers. I recognize Kara's archly lilting voice at once, though she's keeping it low. "You know who I am. It's none of your or any of the others' business what I'm doing when I'm not at the meetings. I don't even know *your* names."

There's a dismissive hiss and a snide male voice that must belong to the rat. "You came to us out of nowhere without warning. We have more reason to be wary of you than you have of us."

I creep close enough through the trees to make out the vague shape of Kara in the darkness. She puts her hands on her hips, lifting her chin so she's looking down her nose at the slightly shorter Murk man. All I can see of him is his pudgy frame and scruffy hair that falls across his shoulders.

"Well, you haven't seen any reason to doubt me here, have you? I have to live somewhere. Do you have a problem with the men of this village?"

The rat shifter scoffs and repeats the word in a sneering tone. "*Village.*" My hackles rise, and I hold back a snarl. He waves his hand toward the clearing. "*You* seem to enjoy their company very much."

Kara's stance goes rigid. "I don't see how that's any of your concern either."

I'm oddly gratified that she doesn't deny her enjoyment or claim it was part of some ruse. But the next remark that falls from her lips sears any particle of relief out of my body.

"I've sworn to contribute my skills to our schemes against the arch-lords. My past actions should more than prove that I have no fondness for the peace treaty. What exactly do you want from me? Or are you only here to harass me for *your* enjoyment?"

Shock scatters my senses, and I miss whatever the rat answers amid the ringing in my ears. I'd wondered what calamity brought Kara to the summer realm, but it never would have occurred to me—for her to be plotting *treason*, working against the hard-won peace that I fought for...

My mind flashes back to our conversation in the common building when she asked me about any lingering animosity toward the ravens. She responded as if she agreed with me that it was better with the war over and all fae living in harmony.

But that must have been an act. There's no denying the declaration she just made. What possible reason could she have to feign being a traitor with this stranger she doesn't even appear to like?

White-hot anger sears through me. I don't let the rage rule me like Ronan sometimes does, but it's time to unleash it anyway. I'll deal with both of these traitors who've brought themselves onto our turf.

My muscles bunch in my shoulders and haunches. Then I launch myself toward the co-conspirators.

I aim for the Murk man first. Kara has already shown how easily she can deceive us. I want to wring some answers out of him before I try her again.

But he jerks around at the thud of my paws and then contracts, shrinking into rat form in the blink of an eye.

I crash down on him, meaning to pin him to the ground regardless. He twitches his body, sending his fur standing on end—and flinging a burst of some foul, magic-laced powder into my face.

The damned rats and their tricks. I snarl, blinking against the stabbing pain in my eyes and nose, scrambling to smack him down under one of my paws. But with both sight and smell temporarily stolen from me, he slips from my grasp. My claws slice through the tip of his tail, earning me nothing but a squeak before he's dashed away.

"Nyle!" Kara says in a choked voice. "Are you all right? What did he—"

I turn toward the sound, braced to spring at her blindly if she tries to flee too. My shift ripples over me so I can speak.

"You're not the one who needs to be asking questions right now, traitor to the Heart."

13

Kara

$\mathcal{W}$hen I finally leave the bonfire and the three men who've conjured so much pleasure in my body, the tension inside me has unwound for the first time all day. I sink down into the bed in my small but cozy house and relax into the mattress. A faint but giddy buzz is still thrumming through my veins, but I don't think it'll take me very long to drift off.

And maybe it wouldn't have if a voice hadn't spoken up less than a minute after I closed my eyes.

"So this is where you've been hiding, Kara of Hazeleven."

I jolt upright, the yelp that would have burst from my lips silenced by a smack of magical force. A stout man bends over me, his narrowed eyes peering at me through the darkness, and I recognize his face and his scent in the same moment.

It's the Murk man I've seen at both of the dissident meetings. My pulse stutters.

How did he find me here? What does he want?

My mind scrambles for any memories of things I might have said that would jeopardize the scheme I've embarked on, but none of my talk with my hosts tonight had anything to do with politics. I've spoken about my feelings about the peace and the rulers of the fae very seldom since I arrived here, and about my past not at all.

That's only a minor comfort. Since the rat shifter doesn't make any move other than studying me, suggesting he's not here to launch an attack, I gesture impatiently toward my mouth.

"No yelling," he murmurs, and dismisses the magic that quieted me.

I don't want to draw the attention of my companions. The last thing I want is to have to explain this intruder in their home.

"What do you want?" I demand under my breath. "What are you even doing here?"

"I'm determining exactly who we're really dealing with," the Murk man replies. "There are many things I'd like to ask you about."

I don't know how to make him leave without making a commotion that would bring the Seelie men into the mix. Pursing my lips, I motion in the direction of the woods behind my cabin. "Let's talk away from the buildings. I don't want to disturb my hosts."

The rat shifter gives me an uncomfortably knowing

look, but I ignore it and clamber out from under the covers when he steps back. Not wanting to wander around in the forest in my nightdress, I grab the loosest of my day gowns and tug it over top, since I also have no interest in changing in front of this trespasser.

He's circumspect enough not to speak as we slip between the trees. For several minutes, we walk silently and carefully, until I don't think there's any chance our voices could be heard from the village. Even so, I keep mine hushed when I turn toward the rat shifter.

"How did you even find me here?" I flew home from both of the meetings, moving faster than a rat could run and watching for carriages nearby. I can't imagine he traced me by scent, unless the rodent has learned how to grow wings.

A self-satisfied smirk crosses his lumpy face. "That's for me to know and you to wonder."

I grit my teeth, resisting the urge to smack the nasty smile off his face. Anger and panic ripple through me in tandem, twisting me in different directions.

How *dare* he slink into my home to threaten me when I've done nothing but appear to support him and his group's cause? How dare he act as if he has any more right to question me than me him?

But he isn't wrong that there are things they don't know about me that it'd benefit them to discover. And if he's somehow figured out how I've been misleading them, I have no idea how bad the backlash will be.

It'll certainly ruin any hopes I had of proving myself a reformed woman, but that might be the least of my problems.

He must have used some Murk trick to track me down. Maybe he cast a little magic on me that I didn't realize during last night's meeting.

That possibility sends a flicker of a different sort of discomfort through me. "How long have you been sneaking around the clearing?" How much has he seen tonight?

The rat's grin turns even crueler. "Long enough to get a very good show. But that wasn't what I came for. Why are you living here, of all possible places?"

I glower at him. "Who says I had that many possibilities?"

He tsks his tongue. "A woman of your high standing and true-blooded heritage would surely be welcome just about anywhere."

He's mocking me. I bite back another flare of anger. "Most of the Seelie haven't been particularly welcoming. I wonder where exactly *you* spend your nights. Have you found them eager to make merry with a rat?"

The shaggy hair that sticks up from his head seems to ruffle as if he's raised his hackles. "We're here to talk about you."

"That's your decision. I don't want anything to do with it. I'd like to go right back to bed."

"You'll answer my questions to my satisfaction first."

I grimace at him. "It doesn't sound as if you have any reason to question me. You know who I am. It's none of your or any the others' business what I'm doing when I'm not at the meetings. I don't even know *your* names."

He lets out a hiss. "You came to us out of nowhere

without warning. We have more reason to be wary of you than you have of us."

I set my hands on my hips, hoping that makes me look more intimidating. "Well, you haven't seen any reason to doubt me here, have you? I have to live somewhere. Do you have a problem with the men of this village?"

"*Village*," the rat shifter sneers, mocking my use of the term for such a small habitation. "*You* seem to enjoy their company very much."

I want to peck his eyes right out. "I don't see how that's any of your concern either." I make my voice even more firm. "I've sworn to contribute my skills to our schemes against the arch-lords. My past actions should more than prove that I have no fondness for the peace treaty. What exactly do you want from me? Or are you only here to harass me for *your* enjoyment?"

The rat shifter wrinkles his nose at me. "We've come too far to risk our plans because of a sudden interloper with big ideas she maybe can't carry through on. I have every right—"

A furry shape springs at him out of the trees so fast it's a blur. I clap my hand over a squeak of shock and stumble backward. The Murk man gulps a breath, already shifting into his small rodent form.

A wolfish body I recognize as Nyle by the scars cutting through the fur on his face crashes over the rat. But the Murk man must pull some trick, because an instant later the wolf is sputtering, pounding his paws wildly as if he's trying to find something he can't see. I catch just a glimpse of the rat vanishing into the shadows.

I could give chase, but I don't really want my Seelie hosts questioning him. And Nyle is shaking his head in obvious distress.

I step toward him, my heart thudding. "Nyle! Are you all right? What did he—"

He whirls toward me so aggressively the words snag in my throat. As he shifts into human form, pressing one hand to his reddened eyes, his voice spills out of him with a snarl. "You're not the one who needs to be asking questions right now, traitor to the Heart."

My whole body freezes, my blood turning to ice. He didn't charge in at the first sight of the Murk man but listened to our conversation first—but then, how could I even have hoped that Nyle would do anything else? He's the coolest-headed of the three men; he appeals to logic and evidence rather than emotion.

And right now he couldn't appear more furious with me.

"I—I—" I stammer, my mind blanking in an even starker panic than the rat shifter's arrival provoked. "I can explain."

Although I don't know how, and I don't know if there's any way I can that will fix this. Dust and doom, I've ruined everything.

Nyle mutters the true name for water and splashes the glob he conjured into his eyes to flush out whatever the rat flicked into them. Swiping at his face, he fixes me with a glare that cuts right through me. "You'll explain in front of all of us. Come on now."

He clamps his hand around my wrist. My pulse hitches.

I have the sudden, wild impulse to flee—to shift into raven form so swiftly he won't be able to catch me before I've soared off into the sky. To leave behind all my belongings and the men who've sheltered me for the past several days. To somehow start all over again, yet again...

The knot that's forming in my gut seems to weigh me down. These men know my name. Now that they have reason to worry about my allegiances, they'll ask around more widely and find someone who'll know of a raven shifter named Kara who had grievances against the arch-lords. And they'll assume the worst.

If word about what Nyle overheard gets back to the arch-lords, there'll be no escaping, no fresh starts. I'll be banished to the most treacherous parts of the fringelands or all the way out to the human world, if they let me live at all.

I made this mess. I need to stay and face it. No matter how much the thought of admitting my past crimes to these men horrifies me.

My horror grows as Nyle marches me back into the clearing and calls for his friends. Ronan and Brice hurry out of their cabins, rumpled but alert at the urgency in his voice. I look from one of them to the next, and my heart only sinks farther, until it feels as if it'll fall right out the bottom of my body and plummet into the earth beneath my feet.

No matter what I tried to tell myself in the moment, what happened between us tonight wasn't a meaningless fling. These three men have come to matter to me in the time I've spent in their presence. I wanted to be worthy of them—I wanted to earn their kindness.

And now I have to admit to them how little I deserve it.

"What's going on?" Ronan asks with a growl that seems directed at the situation in general. He can't know what to make of it yet. His stormy gaze takes in my disheveled clothing and Nyle's manacle of a hand, and his mouth tugs into a deep frown.

"I came upon our guest in the woods, talking to a rat," Nyle bites out, his voice like chilled steel. "Discussing with him how they've been scheming against the arch-lords to destroy the peace treaty."

Brice's eyes widen. Ronan's lips draw back from his teeth, where his fangs have protruded. "*What?*"

I hold up my free hand, spitting the words out as quickly as I can manage. "It isn't true! I—" My voice drops. I doubt the rat shifter has stuck around after Nyle's attack, but I don't want any chance of him overhearing this confession. "I stumbled on a group that's working to undermine the peace. I only pretended I wanted to help them so that I could find out more about their plans and turn them in."

Nyle turns his piercing gaze back on me. "And we're supposed to believe that? Of course you'd make that kind of claim rather than admit to treason yourself."

Brice looks ill. "Why would you even attempt to trick them? If you really wanted to stop them, you could have told us, gotten help."

"And what good would that have done?" I ask, my shoulders slumping. "I've been to two of their meetings, and I still don't know enough about them to identify them or prove they've done anything wrong. Even if I could have found them by touring the villages around here, it'd be my word against theirs. And the arch-lords would never believe *me*."

My lips clamp shut, but I know the moment those words have left my mouth that there's no avoiding the rest of the story. But then, I'm not sure there ever was.

"And why is that?" Ronan asks gruffly.

My gaze drops to the grassy ground between us. It's easier to find the will to go on when I'm staring at that instead of into their accusing eyes. When I don't have to see how their expressions will alter even more as they hear the truth. But it still takes several seconds before I can propel more sound up my throat.

"A little more than ten years ago, during the war with the Murk, I met my soul-twined mate," I say roughly. "It was Arch-Lord Corwin. But he was already wrapped up in a soul-twined bond with Lady Talia, one that the Murk king created with his magic. Arch-Lord Corwin refused me. Lady Talia wouldn't release her claim. I was so upset and frantic I—I made a deal with a Seelie lord who hated her to arrange to have her captured and turned over to the Murk like they were demanding."

The silence that follows is so deafening I wince. Ronan sucks in a harsh breath. Nyle's fingers twitch around my wrist, as if it disgusts him to stay in contact with me but he feels he has to continue restraining me.

"You're that raven," Brice murmurs in a faint voice. "We heard about—you weren't banished?"

My gaze stays fixed on the ground. "My sentence was generous in consideration for the unusual circumstances. I was confined to my home domain for ten years. It would have been longer, but I proved to the arch-lords and Lady Talia that I held no further animosity and regretted my past behavior. Which I do regret. Incredibly so. Spying on the dissidents—it was a way to really make up for the harm I did before. If I can prevent *them* from doing the harm they mean to…"

Ronan shifts his weight on his feet uneasily. "How can we trust that to be true? You could just as easily be deceiving us as them."

I grope for the right things to say to convince them. "I came to the summer realm because people here wouldn't recognize me and associate me with my crimes. Back in the winter realm, everyone knows as soon as they hear my name, if not before… If I'd *wanted* to join up with other fae who had it in for the arch-lords, wouldn't it have made more sense to stay where people knew my history?"

"Or you thought you'd be less monitored here," Brice suggests.

I force myself to raise my eyes. "How about you? Wouldn't it be an extremely stupid plan to settle in with three fae who are considered criminals themselves, who've been cast out of their pack for it, if I was trying to avoid outside suspicion?"

Nyle's voice comes out even harder and colder than before. "What has this all been about? Especially tonight? Were we simply a convenient way to get back at the mate who shunned you?"

I'm so startled by the accusation that my head jerks around so I can meet his eyes. "No. Arch-Lord Corwin has no idea about any of this, so how would that even work? The bond never formed on his side; it was blocked by the one he already had, that the Heart reinforced after they defeated the Murk king. It's faded away to nothing even in me. And he definitely doesn't care what company I keep for other reasons either."

Their expressions remain skeptical. My stomach roils. I need to convince them of this one thing at least.

"I've stayed here even though I could have insisted on leaving because this is the happiest and most welcome I've felt since I ruined my own life. No one wanted me even in the domain where I grew up, where I could have ruled one day. I was afraid to tell you any of this because I didn't want to lose what I've found here."

My voice chokes up. "I realize that I might have lost it all the same. I'm sorry I hid it from you. I'm sorry I'm not anywhere near as good as you thought I was. I only wanted to restore my name… and feel like maybe I *was* good enough to belong with you."

I look at each of them in turn. "You were shunned for reasons it sounds like were far less justified than in my case. Wouldn't you want a chance to correct that if you could?"

"We can't get that chance," Ronan says in a dire rumble. But something has adjusted in his posture. He no longer looks as if he's about to spring at me and rend me limb from limb. That's some small improvement.

He motions his friends off to the side. Nyle hesitates and then releases my arm to stalk over to join the others. I hug myself, holding perfectly still as they carry out their terse discussion in low tones.

They know that outright lying would have strained my connection to the Heart and diminished the magic the source of all our power grants me. But that doesn't mean they'll believe I wouldn't go to those lengths to avoid sanction.

Finally, they turn to face me again. All of their expressions are solemn, Ronan's the sternest of all. But he lifts his chin toward the house Brice made for me.

"You can stay for now. We're all tired, and it's been an… eventful night. But we'll be keeping a strict watch. If you fly off to meet with those traitors again, we'll be informing the arch-lords of your treachery immediately."

I swallow thickly, but his response is the best I could really have hoped for.

"I understand, and I appreciate your patience and generosity. I'll do whatever I can to justify the trust you're extending me."

14

Kara

I walk into the common building the next morning with a hole where my stomach should be. The smell of fried sausage and fresh-cut fruit doesn't lift my spirits, even though my mouth manages to water anyway.

Ronan is just setting the platter of sausages on the table next to a plate of flaky rolls and the fruit. Nyle pauses in the process of tipping the pitcher of water toward his glass, studying me briefly with that typically impenetrable expression, and then goes on to pour his drink.

Brice has his back to me at the table, but his head twitches around at his friend's reaction. He offers me a faint smile that doesn't meet his eyes.

Well, no one has pounced on me with their claws to

my throat yet. I walk over to the table on feet that feel leaden, thoughts spinning in the distant regions at the back of my mind.

Maybe I should have taken off overnight after all? Ended this torture and accepted my fate? Was I kidding myself to think I could have even a shadow of the life I once imagined?

But despite the grimness of my one-time lovers' expressions, I don't want to lose them. Their chill in contrast with their usual warmth—well, when it comes to Ronan and Brice, anyway—sends a pang through my heart with an ache to heal the damage I've done.

The list of my transgressions keeps growing, but I've already tried running away and starting over once. I didn't have anything to fight for before. For a little while here, I found something worth putting myself in danger for. If I give up on even that, I might as well lie down and *let* one of them slit my throat.

So I sit at the end of the table where I'm not all that close to any of the three. Brice passes me each dish without a word so I can add morsels to my plate. I keep my portions small, since the hollow of my stomach is now roiling.

When I've claimed a roll from the last platter offered, Nyle breaks the silence. "We've come up with a way to confirm your story from last night. I'm sure you can understand that if you're going to remain with us without us reporting any of what we've discovered, we need to be sure of what side you're really on."

Ronan lets out a rough grunt of agreement.

I glance around the table, relief and dread trickling

through my gut in tandem. "Of course I understand. How exactly are you going to confirm it?"

Nyle gives a dismissive wave of his hand. "Eat first, and then we'll get to it. It won't hurt you."

I'm not sure I can trust his judgment on that, but even kind-hearted Brice doesn't look concerned, so I do my best not to be either. I dig into the crackly pastry that melts sweet and doughy on my tongue and force down a sausage and a few pieces of a citrus fruit I've never had in the winter realm. The tang washes my mouth clean of the savory flavors, and I find I can't bear to swallow anything else down.

The men have eaten more but at a faster pace. Ronan pushes back his chair with a rasp of the legs and gathers the dishes by magic with a few muttered syllables and a flick of his hand. He sends them off to the counter by the sink where normally I've been handling the washing since I arrived.

I hesitate, and Nyle gets up too, beckoning me over to the lounge room where I slept my first night in their village. All three men walk over there with me, keeping a small but wary distance between us.

Ronan and Brice sit on the sofa with its woolen cushions, and Nyle takes the armchair next to it. He motions for me to take the other armchair that's been set facing them.

I sink into it, my skin creeping with anticipation of the impending interrogation and whatever it might entail. My hands twist together on my lap. "Now what?"

It's Ronan who gives the instructions with his air of gruff authority. "We assume you know the true name for light. Conjure a glowing sphere and hold it steady while you tell us again what you're doing here and how you became involved with that group of traitors."

When I blink at him in momentary confusion, Nyle supplies the explanation. "If you lie and your connection to the Heart is shaken, I expect we'll see it in your ability to hold the conjured light. We'll want answers that are as clear as possible, no responding to questions with more questions or vague claims."

Ah. That's actually a pretty clever approach. And light is among the first true names all fae children learn, so they're not wrong that I've mastered it. Its symbol marks my skin just above my left hip.

"That's fine," I say, my body relaxing a little. It really won't hurt me at all, and since I *want* to tell them the truth, the test will actually work in my favor. If this demonstration allows them to fully believe me, I'll lob around glowing spheres until the end of time.

I raise my hands and murmur the true name. "*Sole-un-straw.*" With focused concentration, I form the energy stirred by the syllables into a ball of light about the diameter of my forearm, good and large so they won't think I'm holding back my strength to try to moderate a lie. I hold it steady between my hands over my lap, low enough that I can still meet the men's eyes over the glowing rim.

"I misled you about my identity when you first came to my aid," I say, figuring it's best to start at the beginning. "My name *is* Kara, but I come from the domain of Hazeleven, which is on the fringes of the winter side of the Mists. During the war with the Murk, Hazeleven was overrun by the rats, and my flock was forced to take shelter near the arch-lords' domains around the Heart. That was the first time I'd seen Arch-Lord Corwin since I'd come of age, and I could immediately feel the pull of a soul-twined bond between us."

"But he refused it?" Brice says quietly.

"He couldn't even feel it." My mouth tightens even though the lingering pain is even fainter now than it was when I left Hazeleven. "*I* couldn't fully feel him the way a soul-twined mate is supposed to. I only had the sense that I should be able to, like something in me was grasping frantically at an extended hand that was just out of reach. His soul was already tied to Lady Talia's because of the Murk king's spells."

"How did Arch-Lord Corwin handle the situation?" Ronan asks with a hint of a growl.

I suppose they want to know that to evaluate just how horribly I behaved. Which was still pretty horrible no matter how you cut it.

I suck in a breath. "He was sympathetic and concerned, and immediately set his coterie to work looking into ways that my stunted bond might be eliminated. He was clear that his loyalty and love belonged to Lady Talia and that he was unwilling to explore any kind of relationship with me. And I took that rejection very badly."

I pause to gather myself, gazing into the golden ball of light for a moment instead of meeting their eyes. The shame of my past actions burns far hotter now than any continuing hurt.

"I don't blame him anymore," I can say in total

honesty. "But at the time, I was furious. I thought if Talia were simply *gone*, then the correct bond would form and he'd want me after all. So I made a temporary alliance with enemies of hers among the summer fae who wanted to appease the Murk king by handing her over to the rats and tricked her to allow her to fall into their hands."

"You expected him to kill her," Nyle says coolly. It isn't even a question, he's so sure of the statement.

I wince, but the light doesn't waver. I have to be honest in this too. "Yes. But as you know, that didn't happen. Her other mates were able to free her, and then she ended up killing the Murk king."

A soft laugh escapes me, echoing the startled bemusement that hit me when I first heard the news. "But if I'd had my way, Arch-Lord Corwin wouldn't have just lost his mate. We might have lost the peace altogether. And it would have been my fault. I acted so selfishly, and I've regretted it even more as it's become obvious how much the peace has benefitted everyone in the Mists."

The men study my sphere of light, which remains as steady as before with no special effort of my own. A wisp of hope rises up in me with the sense that they will judge me fairly.

They're good men. I don't know what misunderstanding got them banished from their pack, but I have no doubt of their motivations. That's why I wanted so badly to earn some kind of place among them.

And that's why I'll say whatever truths I need to, no matter how embarrassing, to regain as much of their trust as I can.

Nyle meets my eyes again. "You were restricted to Hazeleven as punishment."

"I wasn't allowed to set foot outside my domain. And I'd imagine my behavior even at home was monitored by the arch-lords. But I tried to do what I could to show my repentance and contribute to the communities around us, and my sentence was mostly lifted a few weeks ago. I was granted passage through any domains in the Mists other than those of the arch-lords and against their borders."

Brice nodded. "Which is why you came here."

"Yes. My name and the role I played in betraying Lady Talia is most known in the winter realm. I knew I wouldn't be easily recognized here. I wanted to see if I could build some kind of new life for myself without my past always being held against me." A bittersweet smile twists my lips. "Obviously that was too much to hope for. But it wasn't fair for me to keep you in the dark. I'm sorry about that."

"How did you stumble on the traitors in the first place?" Ronan demands.

I swallow thickly. "I felt guilty that you were doing all the legwork trying to find out who'd attacked me. I thought I should contribute too. So I slipped out one night and flew off to a couple of the nearest pack villages to scout around. At the second, I saw a man sneaking off. He seemed to be up to something suspicious, so I followed to find out what. He led me to the dissidents' meeting."

Brice frowns. "And you decided to join in?"

"I didn't mean for them to realize I was there, but they caught me. I told them who I was and pretended I'd come to join their cause because, well, I suspected they'd kill me if they realized I was against them."

The light still hasn't flickered. Nyle's voice comes out perfectly even. "And are you against them, in every way?"

"I am," I say, my own voice a little rough with emotion. "I'm happy we're at peace; I'd like the Mists to stay that way. I never supported the war even when it was happening. I don't wish ill on the arch-lords or Lady Talia any longer. I hope they stay well and safe so they can guard against villains like the ones I was pretending to support. I wasn't even planning to go back after I'd gotten away from the one meeting, but…"

My cheeks flush. Nyle's eyes narrow, but it's Ronan who speaks. "But *what?*"

I look at them in turn. I can admit to this, as foolish as it might make me sound. Why shouldn't they know my true feelings? I downplayed them so much last night to protect myself, but they deserve better.

"I realized I was falling for you," I say softly. "All of you. And I wanted to stay here if you'd have me, whatever that might look like. But you've been so good to me, and I… am not very good, on the balance of it, to put it in the simplest terms. I felt even guiltier about that. I decided that I'd learn enough about the traitors' plans to expose them to the arch-lords, and then I'd have proven I'm a better person now."

My last words fade into silence. The sphere glows on between my hands, its gentle energy tingling against my palms. Emotion has flared in Ronan's eyes, and a more relaxed smile has touched Brice's lips, but I still can't read Nyle at all.

Ronan glances at one and then the other, and appears to determine that they have no further questions. He turns his attention back on me. "Thank you. You can release the magic."

I drop my hands, and the light fades away. The quiet in the room stretches unbearably taut.

"What now?" I have to ask.

Ronan leans forward, his muscles flexing throughout his brawny frame. "I say you lead us to the next of those meetings, and the three of us give those traitors what they deserve."

Brice and Nyle start to nod in agreement, but my body stiffens.

"That won't do any good. It won't fix the problem. They're just the local group, the fae who live in this area of the summer realm. From what they've said, they're coordinating with other groups elsewhere... If we're really going to cut them off at the root, we need to know more."

"Squash one branch and then look for the others," Ronan mutters.

I frown. "You'll get into even more trouble too, won't you? You won't be able to prove that the fae you've just attacked were doing anything treacherous. And you're already outcasts—if it's their word against yours, or there's nothing at all but bloody bodies, you can't be sure your account will be believed."

Brice speaks up quietly but firmly. "I don't mind getting into a little trouble if it protects you from having to deal with them again."

A swell of affection fills my chest. He really feels that way even after what he's learned about me?

But as much as the sentiment makes my pulse flutter, I can't approve of it.

"It wouldn't be a little trouble—it'd be a lot. They're organizing a significant move right now that they want me to help out with. It shouldn't take more than another meeting or two before I have enough details that I'll be able to alert the arch-lords ahead of time and let them catch the traitors in the act. Then no one can doubt what they're involved in, and they can be properly questioned to find the rest of their co-conspirators."

Nyle exhales slowly. "She does have a point. That's how I'd approach the problem."

Ronan bares his teeth. "One of them has already tracked her here. They know where she's living. He was harassing her."

"Then we'll keep up more regular patrols, especially at night," Nyle says. "Her association with us shouldn't affect her safety with them anyway. It isn't as if we're known champions for the peace."

"You *want* her to go off to those miscreants?" Brice demands, unexpectedly fierce.

The interplay of emotions that flash across Nyle's scarred face leave my heart thumping twice as fast as before, but with a heady sort of thrill.

"No," he bites out. "I'd rather she was right here where we can see she's safe. But she isn't a pet we can cage. We're not going to lock her up and insist we know better."

Even he cares that much about my well-being. A lump clogs my throat, but I manage to speak past it. "You shouldn't. It's my risk to take. My reputation that I'm trying to recover. I want to do this for *me*."

Ronan lets out a snarl and pushes to his feet, but when his gaze meets mine, it's smoldering with protectiveness rather than anger.

"I can't chain you. But you need to know that putting your life on the line isn't a requirement of staying here either. You made an awful mistake in an awful situation. I should know how easily that can happen. At least you've found a way to set things right again. If you don't deserve to stay here, then none of us do."

15

Kara

*I*n spite of the men's acceptance, I feel so restless throughout the day that I barely eat after breakfast. By the time I'd normally be turning in for the night, my stomach is gnawing on itself.

I pad across the clearing to the common building and help myself to some bread and cheese from the pantry. Somehow I manage to feel a little guilty about the intrusion even though I can't imagine any of the men denying me food when I'm hungry. I gulp it down quickly, my nerves jumping at the hoot of a nearby owl, and slip back out.

One of the men will be patrolling the boundaries of their territory right now. They divided guard duty up into shifts.

I'm not sure who got the first part of the night, but it

isn't Ronan. As I'm passing his cabin, a muffled huff and the thump of a heavy body rolling over reaches my ears.

I pause, the cooling breeze winding around me and teasing at my hair. A moment later, there's another thump and a rough exhalation. I can't tell whether he's having trouble getting to sleep or meeting troubles in his dreams, but either way he doesn't sound at peace.

A tingle washes over my fingers as I remember soothing his anger the other day in the pasture. I waver on my feet and then walk over to his house.

The door opens silently. I've never been in any of the men's private homes before, but this one looks a lot like mine with the same earthen floor and walls, only larger. The doorway leads into a sitting room that's about the size of the single room in my cabin. Another opening in the side wall leads into the bedroom.

Ronan's scent, manly and musky and tinged with a feral edge, floods my nose. There's no mistaking this home for anyone else's. His seating is upholstered with woolen cushions like those in the common building, no doubt from the sheep he tends to. Even in the darkness, I can pick out mottled patches on the walls, as if they were clawed and then mended.

Wolfish ears are usually too sharp to miss even a stealthy approach. By the time I've reached the bedroom without Ronan hollering at me, I'm sure he's asleep. Asleep and dreaming.

He tosses and turns on the bed as I creep over to it, the sheet tangled around his broad torso. A hint of a growl seeps from his throat.

When I get to the frame, I'm close enough to see that

his claws have emerged from his fingertips, glinting darkly against the pale fabric. His closed eyes squeeze tighter. His lips curl into a grimace. He jerks his hand, slicing thin tears in the sheet.

The sight makes me think of the mended patches on his walls. How often does he lose himself in wildness? How far can it take him?

I don't dare touch him immediately in this state, but I hold my hands toward him and murmur the true name for nerves, willing calmness over him the way I did in the pasture. Gradually, his muscles unclench. He sinks deeper into the mattress, his face relaxing. His claws retract.

As the dream releases its hold on him, his senses come back into sharper alertness. He's only taken a few slow, even breaths before his eyelids rise. His gaze pins me where I'm standing next to the bed.

"You sounded upset in your sleep," I say quickly before he has to ask why I've intruded. "I thought you might appreciate a more peaceful rest."

He grunts, but there's no anger in the response. Then he reaches his arm out to me. "Come here?"

My heart skips a beat. I want to, but I'm also terrified of disappointment—of being disappointed that it doesn't mean what I'd want it to or of disappointing him somehow. But bravery wins out. I push myself forward and climb onto the bed next to him.

Ronan wraps his arm around me and hugs me close to his brawny frame. I'm encased in not just his scent but his heat now, but it feels welcoming rather than suffocating.

I duck my head beneath his chin and let the tension in me unwind. "Thank you."

Ronan makes a dismissive sound. "Shouldn't I be thanking you for soothing my sleep?"

I swallow hard. "I mean, for giving me another chance. For letting me stay." *For believing that I'm more than the worst thing I ever did.*

He strokes his hand up and down my back and nuzzles my hair. "That wasn't a hardship. If anything, you belong with us more now than you did before we knew. At least your mistake didn't come with dire consequences for anyone but yourself in the end."

The remark and the unsettled dream I drew him out of send curiosity tickling through me. "What mistake did *you* make? What exactly happened that turned your pack against you? I know you wouldn't have—"

"That's best left in the past," Ronan interrupts, more gruffly than before. "There's nothing to be done about it, and it doesn't matter here."

"But if you—"

"No," he says, so firmly my mouth clamps shut.

I don't think what he said is strictly true. His past obviously matters in some ways, or it wouldn't still be infecting his sleep and shaping his reactions even during the day. Some horror from his history still has its claws in his mind, and he hasn't managed to shake them.

What could have happened that was so awful and yet not shaken his friends' loyalty in him?

The questions I can't ask nibble at the edges of my mind as Ronan and I simply cuddle on the bed. It isn't long before sleep creeps over him again, his breaths slowing with a hint of a rasp.

His body slackens even more. He eases onto his back, his arm sliding off me.

A very large part of me longs to stay there with him, basking in the affection he's offered me until he has to get up for his patrol. But a more insistent part keeps nagging at me.

These men know all the worst aspects of my past now, but I know barely anything about their history. And they won't share it with me. Ronan is hinting that it's somehow *worse* than what I did.

Have I let myself be misled by momentary kindness when there's rot underneath? It isn't as if I can trust myself to be the best judge of character. I haven't had much chance to exercise those skills.

It's hard to believe that Ronan did anything I'd recoil from. If I knew what happened, then I could simply put the worry out of my mind.

That idea tugs me out of the bed. I shift into raven form to fly out the window, but stop at my own house to scrawl a note just in case the men come looking for me before I return. *Needed to stretch my wings. Will be back before morning.*

Then I take off, soaring high where my scent shouldn't reach whoever's on patrol right now, and point myself toward the first of the two villages I observed on my first night of investigations.

The pack there is obviously fond of their partying, as I was hoping. I spot the lights around the field and catch the strains of rollicking music from a few miles away.

It isn't terribly late yet. Let's see if they're open to unexpected visitors after all.

I land in the nearest stand of trees to shift and walk across the fields to the partiers in my human form. Several of the summer fae glance my way in the middle of their dancing and drinking, but no one looks particularly concerned.

Up close, they don't so much look wild as free. Or maybe I've simply come to appreciate the Seelie wildness more than I did before. The sight stirs none of my previous disdain.

When I've almost reached the table of refreshments, a woman who has an authoritative air strides over with her head cocked at an inquisitive angle. At a glance, I peg her for a member of this lord or lady's coterie—or cadre; that's what I've heard the wolves call their rulers' inner circles. That or someone high up among the pack warriors.

"Hello, wanderer," she says, looking me up and down. "What brings you out this way?"

I offer a meek smile. "I have been wandering some, and I heard the music. It's been a long time since I enjoyed a celebration like this. Do you have room for one more to join in, if that isn't imposing too much on your hospitality?"

She grins. "As long as you make merry and not trouble, you're perfectly welcome. Always good to add fresh partners to the mix."

The other Seelie take me in with subtle sniffs of my scent and gazes more curious than wary. I dip my head in greeting and keep that cautious smile on my face as if I'm assessing my welcome.

A girl who isn't quite of age yet bounds over and offers me a plate with a few delicate pastries, beaming as I sample them. The flavors burst across my tongue, both buttery and tart with tendrils of sweetness.

I glance at her. "Did you make these?"

She nods eagerly. "Do you like them? I don't get to share them with fae from outside the pack usually. And never a winter fae." Her mouth snaps shut as if she's afraid she'll have offended me by acknowledging what I am.

"They're absolutely delicious," I tell her honestly. "Fae all across the Mists would be lucky to get to taste these."

Her smile stretches even wider, and my apprehension starts to fade. I doubt this pack would invite me to build a home with them like the three men I've become entwined with, but I can't forget that most of the Seelie are perfectly hospitable. And everyone likes to have their talents appreciated.

The musicians strike up a livelier tune, and one of the men of the pack appears in front of me with a slight dip of a bow that I think is acknowledging my true-blooded status, as little as it matters these days. "Would you care to dance, lady?"

Why not? I extend my hand to let him clasp it, and he tugs me into the midst of the dancers.

For a few songs, I get swept away in the moment, moving from one partner to another, swaying with the melodies, absorbing the buoyant energy that I really haven't been surrounded by in quite a while. Even if Ronan and his friends attempted a party like this, it wouldn't have the same impact with only three—or four—of us.

But maybe it could be like this for them someday.

Brice talked about how they'd meant to expand the village and invite more fae to join them.

Those thoughts bring me back to my real purpose for coming here. I feel as if I've integrated myself well enough with my hosts by now.

At the end of the current song, I step away from the dancing ground to grab a goblet of duskapple wine. As I sip it, I spot the imposing woman who first greeted me around the edge of the gathering. I amble her way, figuring she's the most likely source of accurate information in this bunch.

"Thank you for the warm welcome," I say. "It's sometimes hard to know how to navigate unfamiliar lands."

"Understandable," the woman says with a light laugh. "And I assume you've come far."

"Yes, although I've been in the summer realm for about a month now."

"A good experience so far, I hope?"

A wild jumble of experiences, good and bad, but I'm not going to tell her that. "This has been one of the best," I say instead, and then pause as if thinking of something. "I wondered—when I was flying nearby, I noticed a few buildings in a clearing, maybe thirty miles west of here. No castle and not so many structures it appeared to be a full pack village, but I got the impression someone was living there. It's the first time I've seen a settlement like that. Is that normal in the summer realm?"

As I've spoken, the woman's expression has tensed. I force myself to keep going with my question, but my stomach is already clenching.

"You'll want to stay away from the fae living there," she says in a dark tone. "They're pack-less. Outcasts. And for good reason."

I raise my eyebrows. "Did they use to belong to this pack?"

She shakes her head. "No. From what I understand, they're from one close to the Heart—I don't remember the exact name. But word of their crimes has spread clearly enough, which isn't surprising, given the nature of those crimes. I'd rather they never settled anywhere close to us, but it's unclaimed territory, so it isn't ours to control."

I have to push my next question from my throat. It comes out quieter than the others, but in what could be mistaken for an eager hush of gossipy enthusiasm. "What did they do?"

The woman grimaces. "The leader of the three, he was the eldest son of one of his lady's cadre-chosen. Apparently he's got a temper like he's cursed even now that the curse is lifted. A few years ago, he went savage and murdered both his father and his younger sister—who was nothing more than a child."

16

Ronan

I wake to the early dawn light seeping through my window and the soft thump of a raven landing on my bedroom floor. As I push myself into a sitting position, the dark bird ruffles its feathers and stretches up into the form of the beautiful woman who's captured so much of my attention in the past several days.

My heart leaps to see that she's come back—it disappointed me when Brice roused me for my turn on patrol and I found myself alone in the bed—but then stutters at the tension marring the smooth lines of her face.

"What's wrong?" I ask, a snarl creeping into my voice automatically. All my muscles coil with the readiness to lunge at whatever might be disturbing her.

Kara gazes at me with a wariness I haven't seen from

her since the early days of her arrival, bracing as if she wants to move toward me but won't let herself. "I flew to visit with one of your neighboring packs tonight."

The snarl in my throat turns into a grumble. "You shouldn't be going off on your own."

"As you've been saying from the start. But you either trust me or you don't. And it wasn't to meddle with the traitors. I—I asked about you." She pauses, guilt and uncertainty crossing her face. Then she only looks haunted. "I heard that you killed your father and your little sister."

Now my heart plummets right through the floor. What's disturbing her is *me*.

I open my mouth and close it again, the words clogging my throat. What can I say to her? How can I even try to justify what I haven't forgiven myself for?

"That's true," I settle on finally.

Kara blinks at me as if she expected me to dispute the accusation. She knits her brow. "How did it happen? I've seen you in a rage—you had your head enough to protect me rather than lashing out at random. Did they attack someone else, or…?"

I swallow thickly at the confusion in her voice. She can't wrap her head around the idea without some deeper explanation. She trusts *me* that much—has faith that I couldn't do anything so heinous.

I can't let myself indulge in her compassion. I don't deserve it.

"It doesn't matter. I bear the full responsibility. I destroyed my family. And I dragged my best friends into ostracization with me afterward. That's how it is."

Kara's eyebrows arch slightly. "I get the impression it was more like they insisted on coming than that you dragged them. And it matters to me what exactly the circumstances were."

I scowl at her. "It doesn't involve you."

"No?" She draws herself a little taller, folding her arms over her chest in an imperious pose. "Haven't I answered every question you asked of me, laid out my whole horrible history for the three of you to analyze and evaluate? You said you accepted me for who I am now, that you still want me to stay. But how can we have anything real here if you won't even admit to me why *you're* here?"

Shame washes over me with a prickling heat. She's right. Her past crimes against the arch-lords and their mate had nothing at all to do with us, but we demanded every detail of that story.

How can I refuse her the same? Of course she'd want to understand.

Am I really balking at talking about it to avoid compassion... or to avoid the judgment she might make of me?

My fingers curl around the rumpled bedcovers that've pooled around my waist. My head sags. "It isn't a pretty story."

"Neither was mine," Kara says tartly, but there's a thread of tenderness in her voice too. She sinks into the armchair in the corner of my bedroom and waits for me to continue.

Her patience makes me even more uncomfortable. I cast about for the best starting point and decide I might as well get straight to the heart of the matter. There's no benefit in drawing this out.

"My father was part of the lady of Saplight's cadre," I say. "And considered by many to be the head of the cadre. I'd trained under him to be ready to serve either within that cadre alongside him if need be or in her true-blooded daughter's cadre whether there or elsewhere. He had one other child with my mother: my sister, Aliffe."

I wet my lips and continue. "My mother fought with all the warriors on the front during the skirmishes with the Unseelie. She was cut down when Aliffe was only seven. It shook my father badly."

Kara's expression has tightened. "I'm sorry."

"It isn't your fault," I say, catching her eyes. I had to work through my harsher feelings toward the ravens years ago when the peace was first instituted. "We made mistakes on both sides, and the biggest villain was that Murk king whose curse made us so desperate to begin with."

She inclines her head in acceptance but still looks pained. I push myself onward.

"Aliffe looked a lot like our mother. Maybe that contributed to however our father's mind got warped. But I found out... A few years ago, when she was fifteen, I caught her crying and got her to tell me what the matter was. We'd been close—I'd helped raise her even more than a brother normally would with Mother gone. But she'd managed to hide this from me for so long..." I sucked a breath through my teeth. "Father had been going to her at night, forcing himself on her."

Kara flinches. The horror of it swells inside me all over

again, thick with revulsion, nearly as searing as when Aliffe first made her sobbing admission.

"It'd been going on for *years*," I said with a growl. "And he was carrying on acting like a devoted cadre-chosen and father all the while. I was so furious and disgusted, I raced right over to confront him. I should have taken the time— I should have made sure Aliffe was somewhere safe— maybe I *wanted* her to see me deliver justice for her."

I press my hand to my forehead.

Kara's mouth has twisted. "What happened?" she asks after a moment, her voice tentative.

"He was in his office. Aliffe followed me in. I told him what I knew and how sick it was and roared at him that he was never going to lay another hand on her. I didn't really have a plan; I'm not entirely sure what I would have done next if he'd accepted my rage. But he must have assumed I was going to cut him down right there or else bring him before our lady with Aliffe testifying…"

The ache in my chest cuts off my voice for a few seconds before I can go on. "He lunged at her. He got to her before I could tackle him and sliced her open so quickly and savagely… I don't know if he was getting revenge for her ruining him by exposing him or destroying the proof or—it makes no difference. He killed her. I was on him in the next instant, slitting his throat, but it was too late to save her."

The room falls into silence. My throat feels raw, as if I've been pushing bits of gravel up it rather than words.

Kara gets up to walk over to the bed. She climbs onto it and tucks herself against me, slipping her arm around my waist, leaning her head against my shoulder. "You didn't kill her. It isn't your fault she died. It's *his*."

She sounds so certain, but her conviction barely touches me. "I acted too hastily. I focused more on my anger than on properly protecting her. And in the end, I wasn't fast enough anyway."

"*Anyone* would have been furious." She lets out a little growl that's much more wolfish than birdlike. "How could your pack punish you for that? Your father deserved to die for what he did—surely they could see that?"

I grimace. "They believe that I went mad and murdered both of them."

Kara pulls back to stare at me. "How could they think that? When you told them—"

"I didn't tell them," I interrupt. "What good would it have done? Aliffe was dead, and so was our father. All the accusation would have accomplished is changing the way people thought of her, making them remember her as something tarnished and defiled."

Kara frowns. "It would have made sure they remembered your father properly—as a vicious deviant who needed to be stopped. And it would have let you keep your place there!"

I lift my shoulders in a shrug. "I had no proof. They might have claimed she'd misconstrued the situation or that I'd misunderstood. I didn't want to drag her name through all that when it could so easily have accomplished nothing anyway."

"So you gave up, even though your banishment was totally unfair."

My gaze jerks to hers, anger sparking in my chest. "I

took the punishment I'd earned. Not everything works out in a way that's 'fair.' You of anyone should know that."

Kara looks back at me for a long moment. Her eyes soften, and she rubs her hand up and down my arm in a soothing motion.

"You know what? That's true. And I wasn't there, so I don't know what the best choices necessarily were. But it's obvious that you've been punishing yourself ever since then, even though you didn't really do anything wrong. You were trying to defend her. You're the kind of man who looks out for people. Look at how much compassion you've shown even me."

I take in the affection on her face and in her touch, and a rush of awe sweeps through me. This woman who has lost so much, and the worst of it through no fault of her own, still has so much compassion for *me*. And if she can see something other than a failure and a monster in me, then maybe I should take heed.

She came back here to listen to my story instead of taking what she heard elsewhere at face value. She believed in the goodness in me even when I refused to explain, while my own pack-kin never questioned their horrible assumptions about my behavior.

Kara has been a villain, and it could be that living with that kind of cruelty has prepared her to better identify the same in others—or the lack of it.

She's exactly what I've needed without my ever knowing it.

I lift my hand to tease it over her hair. "I haven't found that compassion difficult to summon at all."

Her eyes shine so bright at my words that a deeper

longing wakes up inside me. I cup her jaw and draw her mouth to mine.

Kara kisses me back, hesitantly and then more eagerly. My hunger grows like a fire searing through my body. I turn her, tipping her down on the bed and bracing myself over her. My cock twitches with desire, but I don't want to rush this.

She's a special woman, exactly the woman for us. The mate who was supposed to be hers turned his back on her. She needs to know just how much *we'll* treasure her.

So I take my time simply kissing her, melding our mouths together and then delving my tongue between her lips. Her tongue rises to twine with mine. I run my hand down the side of her body, reveling in the contrasts of her, the mix of tart and sweet in her mouth, of softness and strength in her lean frame.

When I've thoroughly worshiped her mouth, I leave it to give my respects to the rest of her lovely face. I kiss and nibble the line of her jaw, the arch of her cheekbones, the slope of her nose. Then I attend to her neck.

At the flick of my tongue over her throat, Kara gasps. Her hands run across my shoulders and down my bare chest, lighting fresh flames as they go.

I growl against the urge to claim her with all I have in a savage surge. Finding the tie down the side of her dress, I ease it open and peel the garment down. Her creamy skin is marked with the true names I saw but didn't give much notice last night, some the same familiar ones as mine, others more obscure though perhaps common among the winter fae.

I dapple kisses across her collarbone and then chart a

teasing path over the slope of one breast. Kara lets out an impatient sound, and I tilt my head to grin up at her.

"You'll get what you need, my treasure. Once I'm done giving every part of you the adoration you deserve."

The doubt that flashes across her face cuts me to the core. I pause to push myself back up over her so I can gaze directly into her eyes.

"Your soul-twined mate lost something when he rejected you. Something incredibly precious. I can't regret that when it means we have you instead, but I'm not going to be finished here until I've cherished you from head to toe."

Kara blinks hard, a liquid shimmer forming in her eyes but a joyful glow melting away the doubt. Her hand rises to trace the side of my face. "Your pack lost something awfully special too, and I intend to make sure you never forget that."

I didn't think I could adore her more, but at those words, my heart just about bursts. I kiss her on the mouth again, deeply and passionately, and then I return to worshiping her breasts.

She squirms and mewls at my attentions, so many gorgeous breathy sounds I want to bottle up for always. But if I have my way, we'll do this again and again for centuries to come.

I work over one nipple with my mouth—breathing hot over it, lapping it with my tongue, rolling it between my teeth—until it's as hard as my cock. My fingers bring the other to the same stiffness. Then I switch sides, repeating the process until Kara is outright moaning.

I sink farther down her body, tugging her dress with

me until she's fully exposed. My mouth marks her belly and her hips, then the curve of her thighs, while the scent of her arousal drives me wild. Finally, I can't stop myself from diving between her legs to suckle her most sensitive places.

Kara cries out with a jerk of her hips. I focus on her clit until she's bucking into my mouth and then curl a finger right inside her. With two, she's grasping at my head with a string of needy moans. Absolutely perfect.

Before, I didn't take her to her release like this. Now, I want to taste her coming. I hook my fingers deeper, finding that particularly potent spot inside, and suck on her clit.

She answers my carnal call with a shuddery sigh and a tremor that runs through her whole body. A gush of arousal coats my tongue as I lap it happily over her slit. Then I'm prowling up over her, shedding my drawers as I go.

Kara spreads her legs as if welcoming me home. As I plunge into her, she beams up at me like a beacon of pure delight.

I extend our pleasure as long as I can with slow, steady strokes, but it's becoming more torture than worship. For both of us, from the desperate pants of her breath. I thrust faster, stroking one hand over her breasts, and she shatters beneath me again with a choked gasp.

She clutches me tighter, and I drive into her again and again without restraint now. It doesn't take long before my balls clench, and I'm spilling myself inside her as if there's no one else I'm ever meant to join with.

For several moments, I rest there over her, coming

down from the highs of pleasure. Then I wrap my arm around my lover and yank the covers up over us.

Kara nestles against me without complaint. Her eyelids droop. She must be tired after her late-night jaunt, and I could use a little more rest myself.

As I close my own eyes, absorbing the warmth of her body and knowing she's soaking in mine as well, our earlier conversation tickles back through my mind. Her anger on my behalf. Her insistence that I should have fought to clear my name and stay in Saplight.

Is it possible she had a point? That accepting the sentence and coming out here had more to do with punishing myself unfairly than taking the consequences I was due?

For the first time since our banishment, I don't immediately recoil from the thought. But it doesn't really matter. I don't want to go back "home." I'm happier here, with my friends and this unexpected guest who's shaken up our world in so many ways, most of them wonderful. I can let the past stay the past.

But while she's entangled with that group of traitors, too much about this precious woman's future still hangs in the balance.

17

Kara

$\mathcal{A}$s I glide after the wolf I'm following to another meeting of the dissidents, my men's voices echo through my mind with the varying shades of disapproval they offered when I told them I was heading out again.

Brice: "You don't need to do this. You don't have anything to prove—to us or anyone else. We can tell the local packs what we already know and let them deal with it."

Nyle: "Getting more mixed up with that bunch is going to end badly. Leave them alone. Let them dig their own grave. I don't want them dragging you down."

Ronan (with a growl, naturally): "You stay here, and I'll go out there and teach them a thing or two about dragging people down."

But after a lot of arguing and insistence, they

grudgingly saw me off—with a kiss from each that's lingered in my memory as much as their words have. They swore that if I'm not back by sunrise, they'll tear apart the realm to get me back. Right now, high on their protective devotion and Ronan's adoring words two nights ago, I don't think the dissident group would stand a chance if it came to that.

But I'd rather it didn't. So I'm taking care, hanging back with my usual caution, letting the wolf lead me to tonight's meeting spot.

As I fly, I peer at the landmarks we pass. Is there any pattern to the places where this group decides to gather? Would we be able to predict where and when the next might happen in order to send authorities after them?

It all looks like a bunch of typical summer-realm fields and forests to me. I suppose the traitors wouldn't have gotten far if they held their meetings anyplace that could point to their presence.

This time the secluded spot they've picked isn't sheltered by trees but by a cluster of steep, craggy hills. My unwitting guide weaves between the mossy stones to a sort of alcove in the midst of the rocky inclines.

As usual, he's one of the last to arrive. A dozen other figures are clustered in the faint light of a pale glowing orb someone has conjured, resting on the ground between them. I conceal myself in the shadow beneath a jutting rock while a couple more fae join the gathering. Then I drift down to the ground and shift.

The mohawked Seelie man gives me a smile that's hard around the edges. "Our raven princess has returned."

I cock my head. "At some point, you'll need to stop being surprised by that."

My gaze slides across the group, pausing briefly on the rat shifter who spied on me a few nights ago. He bares his teeth in a mocking grin but says nothing. I don't know if he's told the others about tracking me down, but there wouldn't be much to tell anyway.

"You missed the first part of the conversation, arch-lord betrayer," the Seelie woman with the patchy hair sneers. "We're already solidifying plans."

I cross my arms over my chest. "You can't expect me to be here promptly when you aren't bothering to tell me in advance where or when the meeting will be."

The Unseelie man steps to the side of the group, eyeing me. "And how *are* you finding your way here?"

I smile thinly at him. "I'm allowed to keep a few secrets to myself, as you all are. But whatever plans you've made, fill me in and I'll help as I've promised."

Mohawk rubs his fleshy hands together. "We were hoping you'd say that. But before we decide how you can contribute, I think we need a demonstration of this nerve-altering talent of yours."

My pulse stutters. Somehow I don't think they're going to ask me to tame a nightmare or ease someone's worries. "What do you mean by that? Are we going on some mission tonight?"

"No, there are plenty of test subjects you can work on right here." The wolf shifter casts his gaze over his fellow dissidents with no evident concern. Whatever he believes about my abilities, he doesn't think I could actually hurt any of them even if I wanted to. "We have to know both the range of your skills and how much power you can put into them."

I can tell I'm not going to enjoy following his orders, but I don't have much choice. If I refuse, then they won't trust me, and I won't find out anything that could expose them to the arch-lords.

Messing with the emotions of these traitors isn't morally repugnant in itself. But I haven't used my skill to provoke anything uncomfortable in another fae since I stirred up Lady Talia's fears while sending her to her supposed doom.

Just the memory makes me queasy. Acting out a similar process will bring those memories into starker clarity.

But why shouldn't I have to relive my past shame to make up for it? How many times will she have remembered her kidnapping with far more horror than I experienced on my end of things?

I roll my shoulders as if warming myself up. "Fair enough. Tell me exactly what you want to see, and I'll get to it."

Mohawk's hard smile comes back. He motions to his companions, and three of the other wolf shifters step forward. They're trying to look tough, but the slant of their lips and the flicker of their eyes suggests they're not entirely happy about "volunteering."

The group's de facto leader obviously arranged for this test ahead of time. I wonder just how much sway he has over the others.

He points to the first of the volunteers, a skinny man. "Let's see how scared you can make him."

My stomach starts to churn, but I hold my chin high and focus on the man in front of me. The true name slips off my tongue, soft and lilting, and my sense of his current emotional state sharpens.

He *is* already a little nervous. That'll make my job even easier. Talia was the same, on edge because of the desperate call I'd made to her and the strangeness of the circumstances. It was so simple to jangle her nerves even more...

I push those thoughts away and focus on the present. They want to see scared? I'll give them terrified. A little advance punishment that's the least they deserve for the schemes they're immersed in.

I speak the true name again and push my will toward the man, imagining the effects I want to create. Adrenaline rushing. Jitters coursing through his body. A sense that something unspeakably horrible is about to descend on him. But there's nothing he can do; nowhere he can run. He's trapped with the terror bearing down on him.

A yelp bursts from the man's lips. He scrambles away, tripping over his feet and landing on the ground with a smack of his ass. The next instant, he's shifting into wolf form, streaking toward the nearest gap between the hills with frantic rasps of his claws over the stone.

I look at Mohawk. His gaze travels from his panicked companion to me, and he nods with only the slightest hint of approval.

I whisper the true name once more and jerk back my influence. The wolf crumples, panting with exhaustion, at the edge of the alcove. Without shifting back, he turns his head and glowers at me with those canine eyes.

As if it's my fault his boss put him up to this.

"And her?" I ask without missing a beat, tipping my head toward the gangly woman who's the second of the supposed volunteers.

Mohawk hums to himself as if thinking it over, as if I should believe he didn't know exactly what he wanted from me before I even showed up. The rest of the dissidents remain silent, a few of them shooting uneasy glances toward their wolf-shifted friend.

"Bring her into a rage," he says. "If you can do that? But not directed at any of us. If she's going to tear into anything, let it not be living."

Oh, he thinks that's a real challenge, does he? I'd *rather* let her savage her fellow traitors, but I can follow his instructions just as easily.

I flex my fingers. "Not a problem."

The process is remarkably similar, faster now that my own nerves are thrumming with anticipation from the work I've already done. I murmur the true name and focus on the energy rippling through the woman's body.

Instead of shoving it toward chilly panic, I will a rush of furious heat through her frame. A deep, scorching rage as if the rocky hillside next to her has offended her to the core.

With a snarl, she hurls herself at the craggy stone face, shifting in mid-leap. Her jaws clamp around a knob of rock and snap it right off; her claws send tufts of moss flying.

I don't wait for Mohawk's signal this time. I can tell when the demonstration has gone far enough. I snap her out of her fury and let her slide down the hill, where she stares up at the vicious score marks she etched into the rock.

The rat shifter lets out a low whistle that manages to sound both awed and mocking. I restrain a glare. The other dissidents shuffle on their feet with growing uneasiness.

Except for Mohawk. He simply looks pleased. He motions to the third volunteer, a portly man with a scar across his forehead. "Don't worry, you're getting the easiest job, friend." Mohawk glances at me. "Can you put him to sleep?"

He might not realize it, but that request is actually the most difficult of the three he's made of me. Provoking someone is easier than settling them down, especially to get them so relaxed they'll slip into unconsciousness. Energy builds off itself and resists being tamed.

But I won't falter in front of these traitors.

I aim my concentration at the man even more narrowly than I did with the other two. The syllables of the true name drop from my lips in steady repetition, sending my soothing vibes to wrap around every inch of his body. Every anxious hitch of his pulse and every uncertain tremor of his nerves must be stilled. Every bit of tension tangled up inside him will melt into a comforting warmth.

A prickle of fatigue climbs my back and pinches my skull. I ignore it, watching the man's eyes droop.

My voice drops even lower. His mind drifts. His muscles uncoil.

His knees give, and he slumps into a heap on the ground. A moment later, a rough snore rattles out of him.

Mohawk chuckles and raises his hands to give me a slow clap that raises my hackles instinctively. But there is at least a little genuine appreciation in his eyes when he looks me over again.

"I think you'll do just fine, raven princess. We have some scouting out to do before we launch our biggest offensive so far. And we don't want to have to deal with any guards while we're there. If you can work that sleepy magic on them, you're in."

"What are we scouting for?" I ask. "What's the big offensive?"

He tsks his tongue at me. "We're not sharing all that until we can be completely sure of you. You've never supported us when it really counts yet. Help us get what we need in two nights' time, and we'll know where your loyalties really lie. If you can stick with us that far, I'd imagine your help with the final gambit will be invaluable."

My stomach clenches. I never wanted to actually take part in any attack they made.

But if all they need is for me to put a few guards to sleep, I won't be *hurting* anyone. They wouldn't bother with that subtle an approach unless they expected to come and go without leaving any harm the pack would notice after the guard awaken.

And once I have these people's trust, who knows how many fae I'll be able to save?

"All right," I say firmly. "I'll give it my all."

18

Kara

"But where are you even going?" Brice asks with a worried twist of his mouth. He glances at me before moving another of his conjured earthen blocks onto the growing frame of the cold-sauna he's been building for me. With a flick of his hand, it floats onto the wall that's now as tall as my shoulders.

I sigh. "I don't know yet. They wouldn't tell me. All I have is the meeting spot, and I'm sure they'll be watching closely to make sure I haven't brought anyone with me." I give him a pointed look in case he was thinking of stealthily tagging along.

His huff of breath suggests I wasn't wrong. "I don't like it. Who knows what they might be planning, even if they say it's just preparations for a larger move later?"

"It's better for the fae they're spying on if there's

someone there who cares what happens to them." I offer him a crooked smile. "And one of the benefits of being Unseelie is that I can fly away. If things start looking dire, I'll take to the sky—and sound a warning to the pack as well."

A cooler voice carries from behind me. "As long as they don't blast you out of the air again."

Nyle walks over to join us, looking Brice's structure up and down with an inscrutable expression before focusing on me.

"I'm going to be particularly careful about how easy a target I make now that it's happened once," I inform him.

He simply hums to himself. Then he steps up to the entrance to the cold-sauna. "Let's see how this experiment is working out. The walls should be high enough to have some effect by now."

"It's not really a fair test," Brice protests, but he tramps into the building after his friend.

I'm not going to be left out of the first trial run of the building that's mainly meant for me. I slip in after them.

Brice has made the structure large enough that it's not crowded even with the three of us. They could host several winter fae in here before it got cramped. There's no furniture yet, so we sink down onto the packed earthen floor by the far wall and lean back against the blocks.

The summery sun still glances across the space through the open roof area, streaking light over the entrance. But where we sit in the shade, a mild chill wafts out of the blocks around us. It winds around my limbs and teases a tension from my chest that I hadn't realized was there.

I exhale in a rush and relax into the wall behind me,

closing my eyes. A pang of homesickness jabs through my chest.

It's been so long since I really felt the refreshing but comforting chill of a perfect winter day. This doesn't quite capture it, but it comes close already.

"It's perfect," I tell Brice. "And I'm sure it'll be even more perfect when it's finished."

Nyle shifts his position against the wall with a rustle of his clothes. "There is something to be said for changes of pace. And coolness can bring mental clarity."

Even with my eyes shut, I sense the movement of Brice's head as he turns it to look at me. "Do you really prefer this temperature that much more the climate we have here? The rest of the village isn't *that* uncomfortably hot, is it?"

"No. Sometimes I enjoy the warmth. It's just not what I'm used to. There's something reassuring in familiar sensations." I pause and blink so I can meet his gaze. "Aren't there things you miss about the place where you grew up?"

It's Nyle who answers, with a rough snort. "Not so much that I'd try to recreate them."

"I was asking Brice," I say tartly, and focus on the man next to me again, knitting my brow. "Ronan told me the whole story, you know. About what happened with his father. You knew it couldn't have happened the way people assumed—you stuck with him, all the way out here. Did you feel as unwelcome in the pack as it sounds like Nyle did?"

Brice's gaze flicks toward his friend as if he thinks Nyle might jump in with another snarky response, but the other man simply raises his eyebrows. Brice's mouth twists. He looks down at his hands, raising on his bent knees.

"It was complicated," he says. "I was the son of the lady of Saplight."

I can't help staring at him. "What?"

He shrugs. "It didn't mean much. You can see I'm not true-blooded. I had a much older sister who was the heir. Mother hadn't had any other children, and after a while her mate encouraged her to have relations elsewhere to fill out the family. My father was human, someone she had a quick interlude with outside the Mists and never saw again."

"But still…" He'd have grown up not *that* differently from how I did. Living in a castle rather than in the village with the regular fae. At least somewhat privy to the conversations of rulership. And: "You were going to be on your sister's cadre like Ronan would have been?"

Brice's smile gets even more slanted. "In theory. I've never been much of a warrior or a strategist, so I'm not sure how much use I'd have been."

"You'd have done plenty more than half of those maggot-brains already circling the castle," Nyle mutters.

Brice lets out a rough chuckle. "I'm good for morale. That's what my sister always said. She meant it as a compliment, but when that's the best compliment you can give…"

"I think it's important." I glance at Nyle. "Were you training for—or in—the cadre too?"

He shakes his head. "Nah, I wasn't considered worthy of that. But I was around this one and Ronan plenty because Lady Siobhan and Lord Herold took over raising me. My parents died when I was still young. And then I helped raise him, as much as I managed to get anything to sink in." He flicks Brice's hair, a glint of brotherly mischief lighting in his eyes that softens the scarred planes of his face.

I can almost see them loping around the castle, coming up with boyish schemes together, defending the pack as need be, celebrating when there's nothing to fend off. But it was just the three of them sticking together. For more than a century, if I'm estimating Brice's age right.

I study him again, the question sticking in my throat before I force it out. "You really didn't leave behind much of anything you'd miss? You must have— Being the brother of the lady heir, even if not true-blooded, you'd have been in high demand as a mate."

Brice's expression relaxes. "Maybe a little. I was seeing a woman when the disaster with Ronan and his father happened. But we weren't making any promises to each other yet, and she immediately assumed the worst of Ronan even though he was my friend, so I knew I wasn't losing much by leaving her."

He leans in and nuzzles the side of my head. "And I'm glad, because now we've caught you."

Even as my skin flushes at the affection in his voice, I can't stop myself from pointing out, "You didn't exactly have to *catch* me. I essentially fell into your laps."

Nyle reaches to stroke his fingers up and down my bare shin. The mischief lingers in his eyes, sparking hotter. His tone carries enough heat to melt me. "Would you like to be chased, Kara?"

It isn't a question I've ever asked myself before, but an

eager shiver ripples through me at his words. He must feel it, because his grin widens. "I think you would."

The half-finished building no longer feels at all cool. Brice's voice drops as he nips the shell of my ear. "I think we could satisfy that urge. Our woman deserves a chase. Show her just how much she's wanted."

Is that why the idea appeals to me? I don't even know. I'm just starkly aware of the desire flooding my body. "It's not much chasing if I'm already right here next to you," I murmur.

Nyle traces his fingers around my knee by the hem of my dress. "Hmm. Then I suppose you'd better run so we have a little more of a challenge."

When I get to my feet, my legs are oddly shaky, maybe because of the frenetic thump of my heart. Brice and Nyle stand up as well, their expressions turning giddyingly predatory. I wet my lips and step out of the cold room.

In the clearing, I hesitate. Ronan's recently gone off to make a trade with another pack, so we won't disturb him, but I don't want to startle his livestock. I'd rather not run toward the spot where I was attacked either, with the memories tied to that moment.

So I set off toward the woods on the opposite side from the cold-sauna, my steps picking up speed as I go.

I don't hear the men behind me until I've reached the first trees. There's a rustle and a playful bark, and I know they've taken on their wolf forms. That's when I push my legs into a run.

I may be more suited for flight than racing, but I'm steady enough on my feet when I need to be. I hurtle forward across the uneven terrain, weaving between the trees, the thrill of the moment blazing through every nerve. It sizzles hotter at the sound of paws thundering across the terrain in pursuit.

There's no way I can outrun a wolf. If I really wanted to get away, I'd release my wings and soar off. But all three of us know that's not the point of this diversion at all.

I dodge a jutting rock and leap over a mass of tree roots. The wind rushes through my hair, tossing it over my shoulders. Then, just as I reach a small glade that's grassier than most of the rest of the forest floor, one of the wolves pounces.

It's Brice—I can tell from the nutty tang to his feral scent right as his paws smack around me. He manages to roll so we fall together, me crashing into his furred chest rather than the hard ground. As the breath jolts out of me with a gasp, Nyle springs into the glade to pin me between them.

One instant they're wolves, the next they're men, running their hands over my body. But they've left their claws and fangs intact. Brice rakes his claws down the front of my dress, shredding it off my body, while Nyle teases the tips of his pointed teeth over the sensitive skin at the side of my neck.

I arch between them, wrenched by need. I feel as if I'd have to peel off my skin to get close enough to them.

The fabric falls away from my chest, and Brice dives in to suck the tip of my breast into his mouth. He flicks the very tips of his claws over the other nipple a moment later, and the twin jolts of bliss have me whimpering.

Nyle tests his teeth against my bare shoulder and yanks the rest of my dress away. His hand trails down my side to my thigh and grips my hip with a prickle of his own claws. He presses against my back firmly enough that the bulge within his trousers nudges my bottom.

I rock against him, and he groans. His fangs dig into my flesh just deep enough to puncture the skin. The pain mingles with pleasure in a heady sensation I've never experienced before.

I snatch at Brice's trousers, which are in easier reach. He wriggles out of them without releasing my breasts. His cock juts out just as rigid as Nyle's felt. When I wrap my hand around it, his breath stutters over my nipple.

Nyle delves his hand between my legs from behind, retracting his claws as he does, and massages my sex. I moan and sway with his motions, more need building in my core with a desperate burning.

The way Ronan cherished my body the other night was exquisite, but right now I want to be ravished. I want all the wildness these wolfish men can offer.

The two of them appear to feel the exact same way. Brice captures my mouth and rubs the head of his cock along my inner thigh.

"She's ready for you, whelp," Nyle says in a darkly teasing voice that nearly makes me explode as his breath brushes my ear. He eases my legs farther apart to open the way for his friend. "So wet you could drown in her."

"And what an incredible death that would be," Brice murmurs with a strained chuckle. He lines himself up and plunges into me, all the way to the hilt in one thrust.

My slick channel stretches to encompass him, tingling with the most delightful burn. I hook my higher leg over his and urge him on.

As I press into Brice's thrusts, he lavishes my neck with kisses and nips. Nyle nibbles my shoulder blade and then dips his fingers between the cheeks of my ass. At the brush of the tips over my back opening, another thrill quivers through my nerves.

I feel him smile against my shoulder. "Think you can take me too, darling raven?"

A strangled sound of encouragement seeps out of me. "Yes," I manage to gasp out. "Please."

He murmurs a true name that turns his fingers as slick as my sex. Sliding them over my back entrance, he massages the muscle there. The blissful sensation swells through my pelvis, heightening the pleasure that's already racing through me with Brice's cock slamming home.

By the time Nyle pushes his shaft into me from behind, I'm tingling from head to toe.

"That's right," he growls. "You feel so good, Kara."

The feel of him entering me, sliding inside until I'm doubly full, makes me moan and shiver. Bursts of pleasure rush through my veins like leaves whipped up in a whirlwind. As he and Brice press into me in tandem, again and again, I'm tossed higher and higher, up toward the sky—

And then the bliss takes me in one roaring blaze, searing away my vision and shocking a cry from my throat. The men thrust into me madly and seem to come as one being, tensing with their release on either side of me.

I come back to earth nestled between the two men, who've gone tender now that the urgency of the moment has passed. Nyle leans over and tilts my head toward him to claim a gentle but insistent kiss. Brice pulls me close against him and nestles my head under his chin.

"You're ours now, beautiful one," he states, firm and almost defiant. "We'll be ten times the mate that feather-brained arch-lord would have been."

"Which makes thirty times in total, since there are three of us," Nyle remarks, smugly amused. He gives my neck one last nip. "But he's right. You're not getting rid of us now."

"I wouldn't want to," I mutter, but their words light a flame of joy in my chest.

Of course, our fate may not be up to any of us depending on what the dissidents have in store for me tonight.

19

Kara

The moon is a pale crescent in the sky when I reach the meet-up place: a little grove of trees on the bank of a narrow river about four hours' flight from my new home. I land on a branch and peer through the shadows between the trees.

No one stirs for several minutes, though I can taste wolfish scents in the air. One of the dissidents must have used magic to conceal their presence. But after a time, they clearly decide I haven't brought any kind of doom with me, because three of the Seelie, including Mohawk, guide a small wooden carriage out into the open.

Mohawk glances my way and nods, the first time any of them have acknowledged my presence. I leap down toward the carriage, transforming just in time to land on human feet. I sink primly onto the bare bench in the middle and glance from the two at the back to Mohawk at the front.

"Just the four of us?" I ask as the woman behind me motions for the carriage to take flight.

Mohawk smiles thinly. "For now. We catch less attention traveling separately."

Yet he felt he needed two wolves as backup to pick me up. Was he really that concerned that *I'd* bring some kind of backup with me? If he distrusts me that much, I'm surprised he's bringing me along at all.

I glance across the shadowed plain, the wind whispering past my ears as it teases through my hair. "Are you going to tell me where we're going now?"

He makes a noncommittal noise, but he does answer more than he has before. "It's a domain not too far from the arch-lords' homes. I think it'll give us some necessary perspective."

"Because for now we're only just looking around," I say, phrasing it as a statement but leaving it open for him to correct me.

His smile widens just a tad. "Exactly. A simple scouting mission. But we wouldn't want the pack sentries interfering with it. And it's the perfect chance to confirm that you can act when the pressure is on."

Lucky me. I ignore the prickle of apprehension that runs down my back.

He said this domain isn't "too far" from those of the arch-lords', but I'm only forbidden from visiting their nearest neighbors. We're still at least a hundred miles distant from the Heart itself, its energy the faintest of thrums in the air. And if Mohawk is planning on taking us closer than my vows will allow me, then I'll just have to use them to beg off.

He can't point to the sanctions to question my loyalty. The only reason I'm forbidden is because of my past crimes against the men he wants to screw over too.

The carriage moves swiftly, but we travel for less than an hour before Mohawk motions to his companions to slow it. The woman directs the craft through a dense forest, all of the Seelie peering between the trees in watch. I have no idea what they're looking for, and none of them is inclined to tell me. When I open my mouth to ask, Mohawk presses his finger to his lips.

After several more minutes, he motions for the carriage to halt completely. Then he points to me and beckons me closer.

"There's a sentry on patrol a minute or two due north of here," he murmurs by my ear. "Fly over there and work your sleepy magic on him. Let us know when it's done."

My stomach clenches, but I nod as if his command is of no concern at all. With a shake of my shoulders, I push off from the floor of the carriage and contract into my raven form.

In the air, I catch the scent of an unfamiliar wolf coming from the direction Mohawk indicated. I glide toward her, barely flapping my wings, silent as a shadow. Then I spot a furred form moving through the underbrush.

The sentry pauses to sniff at a bush. I drift down onto

a thick branch, performing the softest of landings, and hunch so that I shift back in a crouch, my hands gripping the bark for balance. Training my attention on the wolf below, I murmur the true name under my breath so faintly it's little more than a breath.

Loosened nerves, slackening mind. Tension unraveling, alertness melting. Let go of all thought. Let go.

The process takes longer than with my earlier test subject—more repeated intonations of the true name, more concentration—before the wolf sinks down on her belly, lays her head on the ground, and finally gives herself over to sleep. That's not surprising, considering she was specifically at work, needing to stay alert. She was a good sentry.

A pinch of guilt follows me back to the carriage. "It's done," I whisper to Mohawk.

He gestures to one of his companions. The other man slinks off the carriage in wolf form, trots away, and returns a minute later. As he straightens up again, he gives a nod. "The sentry's sleeping like a pup."

"Excellent." Mohawk flashes his teeth at me in a grin it's hard to take as friendly before he urges the carriage forward again. But I've relaxed a little. The other man couldn't have said that unless he left her asleep rather than doing something worse.

They really do just want to sneak in and out again without disruption.

I get the impression that we're circling around the domain now rather than heading into it. We come across two other sentries, whom my companions have me put to sleep the same way as the first. By the third, a splinter of a headache has woken up at the base of my skull.

Nerves might be my specialty, but that doesn't mean I have infinite magical strength. This is difficult work.

To my relief, the third appears to be the end of them. The carriage swerves in a different direction. Mohawk brings the vehicle to a stop in a small grove and hops out, motioning for the rest of us to follow him.

We walk in silence to where the trees thin at the edge of a vast field dotted with flowers so vibrantly blue I can make out their color even in the dim moonlight. Their cloying perfume fills the air, making my nose twitch.

We've emerged by the side of the castle that stands a couple of minutes' walk from where we're poised. Beyond it lies the pack village, most of those buildings hidden behind the sprawling two-story structure that looks as if it's formed out of some kind of metal. Mohawk peers around the field and then turns to us, his voice pitched low.

"Raven, you stay here and keep watch for anyone stirring. The rest of us will make our observations. Stay still and silent unless you need to act."

"Of course," I mutter, crossing my arms over my chest.

My whole body is tensed with uneasiness. I haven't seen any of the other dissidents yet—are they even here or did Mohawk deceive me for some reason about them joining us? Or does he not even want me to see how they arrived or what they're doing?

I'm still far too much in the dark.

The three Seelie shift into wolves and lope off. I slip back into my raven form and perch on the branch of a tree, high enough to make out most of the field before me. I catch a few glimpses of the wolfish shapes blending in and out of the shadows, but they're skilled at stealth. If I didn't know they were there, I'm not sure I'd have noticed them.

I could try to alert the leaders of this pack now and hope they catch the traitors doing something incriminating enough to warrant capture. But I don't know how closely *I'm* being watched. Maybe one of the dissidents is keeping an eye on me even now, judging my loyalties. If I fly off from my assigned role, the others might be alerted before I can sound the slightest alarm.

It's not worth the risk unless I'm sure they're committing a particularly grievous crime right now.

No one stirs throughout the village. The pack is counting on their sentries to alert them to any danger. And they probably weren't all that worried about danger to begin with. The war is supposed to be over. We're at peace with our neighbors.

The traitors I'm pretending to be allied with want to end all that. How can they think chaos and violence is the better option? Even when I threw Lady Talia to the wolves, it wasn't because I had any fondness for the war. I simply wanted my soul-twined mate to be mine.

For perhaps half an hour, I wait there, every sense alert, every nerve on edge. But when nothing happens that requires me to dive in, I relax just a little. I ruffle my feathers and briefly stretch my wings, wondering how long Mohawk's "observations" are going to take.

Then, without warning, a force slams into my raven body from behind.

It isn't like the blast of magic that brought me to my three outcast men. There's no searing of pain and no heat, just a sensation like a brutal shove, propelling me forward.

It smacks me right off the branch, head over heels. My wings shoot open with desperate flaps to right myself; I clamp my beak shut against a startled croak.

Before I can whirl around, another blow hits me, and another, tossing me farther across the field. My head spins with dizziness. My throat starts to ache.

Should I give some kind of warning to my supposed allies? But that would wake the pack. What is even happening?

After the sixth smack, I stretch into human form. My sudden weight brings me tumbling to the grass.

I roll among the flowers and scramble up, and a figure dashes by. I think I make out the patchy hair of the Seelie woman who's an outspoken member of the dissidents right before she hurls a large sack at me.

A few items I can't make out spill from the sack's open mouth and bounce off my body to hit the ground with a heavy clatter. A voice calls out from somewhere behind me, shouting in alarm.

I shove my hair back from my face, totally disoriented, and realize I'm standing just a few paces from the castle. The strange attack propelled me that far.

I whip around, meaning to launch myself into the air to escape, but a wolf leaps out of the darkness. It tackles me to the ground, knocking the air from my lungs.

More shouts ring out all around me. What in the realms is going on?

My instinct is still to shift and fly, but the wolf who's

pinned me clamps her jaws around my forearm, not quite digging into the flesh. I know if I tried to transform, she'd chomp right down on my wing, and I'd get nowhere.

Light glares down on us. Someone has conjured a few glowing orbs. Seelie have gathered all around me. A few are pawing through the objects that fell from the sack Patchy tossed at me. My gaze flicks over the mess, and with a lurch of my heart, I spot a dagger. A vial that's ominously red. Some kind of twisted hook.

Those don't look like the sorts of things you'd bring as a hostess gift on a friendly visit.

A sinking sensation grips my gut. My mouth has gone dry.

They set me up. For some purpose of their own, the dissidents have turned me into a scapegoat. Whatever else they did here tonight will no doubt be blamed on me. And how can I tell anyone I'm innocent with the history I've got weighing me down?

I can't help trying anyway. "I didn't mean to do anything wrong. None of this is mine. I—"

"Be quiet, raven traitor," one of the Seelie men snaps, and then stiffens to attention. Casting my gaze in the direction he's looking, I get my first glimpse of the lord of this pack, striding around the side of the castle with a regal air and a disgruntled expression.

"What's going on out here?" he demands.

"I can ex—" I start to say, and my captor slaps her hand over my mouth to cut off my offer of an explanation.

"We caught this Unseelie woman lurking here by the castle," another of the wolf shifters says in a growl. "It looks like she was attempting some kind of stealth assault on the pack."

The lord glowers down at me, his face hardening even more than before. "Send word to the arch-lords. They'll want to hear about this."

20

Brice

$\mathcal{N}$ormally, a dawn this bright would lift my spirits. But my emotions are too tangled up with worries about Kara for me to appreciate the brilliant start to the day. I haven't been able to sleep for the last couple of hours, and my rest before that was wrenched by erratic nightmares.

I peel myself off the bed, splash some water on my face from the basin to wake me up more, and hurry out of my cabin to check on her.

My rap on her door brings no answer. My stomach clenching, I ease it open.

Her bed is empty, the covers pulled straight and neatly tucked. The coolly sweet scent of her that lingers in the space has grown fainter overnight. She hasn't been back.

I inhale slowly, willing back the surge of panic. Her

absence doesn't mean anything has necessarily gone wrong. She didn't know exactly what the dissidents' plan involved. It's possible they were busy for the whole night, and she simply hasn't had time to make it back yet. The meeting point she told us about was a pretty long flight away.

But if something *has* gone wrong, how would we even know about it?

I back out of the cabin and move toward the common building, but I can't settle my mind enough to even think about breakfast. I end up pacing around the clearing, my muscles tensed all down my back, the urge to let out my wolf and hurtle through the woods itching at me.

But I have no idea where Kara even went after she reached the meeting point. I have no idea what direction she might be returning from.

I'm at least as likely to pass her by as to find her.

It isn't long before Nyle emerges from his cabin, sharp-eyed as usual despite the early hour. He takes one look at me and frowns. "I take it she's not back."

I shake my head. "No sign of her."

He lets out a breath and flexes his muscles as if releasing tension, but his voice goes taut. "She did say she'd send a message if all was well but she couldn't return by morning. It's barely morning now. That message could be on its way already."

I don't slow my pacing. "And if it doesn't come? How long do we wait?"

"What are we going to do *other* than wait?" He pauses. "There's also always the chance that she adjusted her loyalties after all, and she doesn't *want* to come back."

His suggestion startles me so much that I jar to a halt.

I spin on him, my eyes narrowing. "You don't really believe that after everything she said, do you? She wasn't lying. By the Heart, even without your test with the light, you had to be able to hear how much she meant it. And yesterday…"

Nyle's mouth slants just slightly, the only outward sign he lets show that he's as disturbed by the idea of Kara abandoning us as I am. "I'm not saying she lied. I'm saying we don't know how deep her convictions ran or what the traitors might have said to her and shown her. If she saw a definite chance of getting her soul-twined mate after all—"

Oh, is that what his doubts are about? My friend has a keen, steady mind about almost everything, but he does falter in a few areas.

I stride over to him and grip his shoulder. "She wanted *us*. She was done with the arch-lord. She told us how much we mean to her, and we showed her we feel the same."

Nyle gazes back at me evenly, but the twitch of his jaw betrays his insecurity. None of the women of our old pack ever saw him as worthy of more than a quick roll-around. But I've never seen the slightest hint that Kara minds his scars, and she certainly doesn't give a badger's ass about our social standing, considering she's known we're packless from the start.

"We can't comprehend the power of a soul-twined bond," he reminds me. "It's not something that's ever been in the realm of possibility for any of us."

With a rustling of the underbrush, Ronan emerges from the forest, done with his patrol. He takes in our tensed stances, probably having heard our last few exchanges or at least the terseness of our voices, and frowns. "What's this about?"

I grimace. "Nyle thinks Kara might have thrown us aside to chase after her arch-lord again." My gaze jerks back to Nyle, just shy of a glare. "The only way that could happen anyway is if Lady Talia died. You heard how horrified Kara is by what she tried to do before. I can't think of any reason she'd be a party to a plan that would harm someone again."

He opens his mouth as if to argue, but no words come out. Instead, he swipes his hand over his face. "We don't know her that well," he says finally, but his tone isn't convincing.

I think at this point he's simply switching into self-defence mode. Easier to decide now that we didn't mean enough to her and harden himself to any possible hurt. I can't let him dismiss the woman who's made herself ours, though.

I know her. I felt how nervous she was that we didn't return her affection for us. How eager she was to receive everything Nyle and I offered her yesterday.

She could have fled from us when we realized the truth about her situation, but she stayed. She admitted her shame because she'd rather we know than lose us. She was more willing to admit what she'd done than Ronan was, even though her crime was worse.

"Don't," I tell him with a firmness I don't usually bring to bear, channeling my mother, who I watched lay down the law with the pack so many times. "If she doesn't make it back soon, then something's dragged her away from us against her will, and she'll need our help. Don't you dare turn your back on her when she never did with us."

Nyle stares at me for a second and then averts his gaze, chagrinned. "I didn't mean—I'm sorry. This is a situation we've never navigated before."

Fair enough.

Ronan stirs restlessly on his feet. The sun has already risen higher over us as we've been talking. "How long do we wait before we take action? We don't want to jeopardize her cover."

I consider, the twisting of my gut urging for swift action, my more measured thoughts calling for caution. "We should make some breakfast and eat as well as we can, and then handle the basic morning chores. That should bring us to mid-morning. If she hasn't gotten word to us by that point, I think we have to assume something's preventing her and we need to intervene. The only question is how."

"We'd have to go to the arch-lords," Nyle says quietly.

Ronan's head jerks toward him. "What?"

The other man picks up conviction as he goes. "If the traitors were caught with Kara among them, the incident will have been reported to the arch-lords. We don't know where the bunch of them are now, but the arch-lords will. And if it's the traitors holding her, then the arch-lords need to be warned about them regardless. They have the resources to find them—we don't."

His explanation makes perfect sense. All the same, I'm not surprised by how rigid Ronan's stance has gone.

"The arch-lords won't listen to anything we have to say," he says in a rasp. "They'll have heard about our banishment—probably a great deal, considering Lady Siobhan and Lord Herold socialize with them regularly. Why would they believe anything a miscreant who murdered his own father and sister or the friends who stood with him have to say?"

I drag in a breath, discomfort tangling around my gut alongside a sense of resignation. So, this is how that lingering thorn in our sides finally becomes unavoidable.

We've ignored the shadow hanging over us for so long, as if it will simply vanish if we don't talk about it, but here it is, turned solid and blocking our way.

"You didn't murder your sister," I remind Ronan. "And you can tell them that now just as easily as you could have told my mother back then."

His lips pull back from his teeth, where his canines have sharpened just slightly with a hint of his fangs. "Aliffe shouldn't—"

To my surprise, Nyle breaks in before I have to. "Aliffe won't care. She's gone. She's been gone for years, her spirit passed on into her soulstone."

Ronan looks at him with a betrayed expression. "*You* think we should go back and beg for a second chance?"

"No," Nyle says shortly. "I don't want anything to do with Saplight or its pack again. But that doesn't mean we have to let everyone go on believing you're some kind of rabid animal."

"It doesn't matter to me what they think of me," Ronan growls. "I don't want them thinking of Aliffe that way."

I can't keep quiet any longer. "What about how they'll think about Kara? If she was caught supposedly helping the traitors or if we have to say she's being held by them, do you really think anyone will believe *her* that it was all a double-cross, no matter what she says? The woman she tried to kill is one of our arch-lords' mates as well, in case you've forgotten."

"We'd hardly be helping her case if they find out she's been associating with us too."

I plant my hands on my hips and stare the older man down. I've accepted Ronan's authority without question in almost everything my whole life. He's been a constant, steady presence since I was a pup. But he has his failings just as Nyle does.

I might not be as quick-witted as Nyle or as strong as Ronan, but I know right from wrong.

"Only because of what they currently believe about you," I say. "And we could turn that around. I know you're protecting Aliffe's memory, but is it really worth hiding what happened to her if keeping silent means condemning Kara? Who really matters more, Ronan: the girl who's dead or the woman who's still alive, at least as long as the fae who'd punish her are merciful?"

There's a moment of silence so heavy even the chirping of the forest birds seems to dull. Ronan's jaw works. Then he lowers his head.

"You're right. Our woman deserves better than that. If she's in trouble, we have to fight for her whatever way we can."

His chin comes up again, a flare of determination lighting in his eyes. "We should leave now. It'll take a while to reach the arch-lords' domains. If Kara has sent a message our way, it'll be keyed to us, not the buildings.

It'll find us, and then we can turn back. But if it doesn't come… we should speak for her as soon as we can."

My heart leaps with relief. A small smile curls Nyle's lips. And with that, we spring into action to save the woman we've all fallen for, wherever she might be.

21

Kara

or all the differences between the summer and winter realms, the prison cells on both sides are remarkably similar. The hard stone floor and barred door of the one I'm sitting in now brings back uncomfortable memories of the Unseelie jail I was shut away in ten years ago while the arch-lords debated the appropriate punishment for my crime.

One of the fae in the domain the dissidents targeted knocked me out with magic before transporting me here, so I'm not sure whose prison I'm in. Presumably one of the Seelie arch-lords'. Also presumably not Arch-Lord Sylas's, since I doubt he wants me in the same building as his shared mate, given that she was the target of my last actual crime.

That leaves the rigid older woman who often seems

like she'd fit in nearly as well as a cool-headed raven or the young man with the flame-like hair that matches his warmer temperament. If I had the choice, I'd go with him, but it isn't as if anyone bothered to ask my preference.

I don't even know how long I've been down here. I woke what feels like hours ago, and my stomach was clenched with enough hunger that I immediately gulped down the basic meal of bread and cured meat that had been left on a plate next to me. The jar of water that accompanied it is down to its last couple of inches. I've had to resort to relieving myself in the bucket in the corner.

Who knows how many more times I'll need to use that bucket while the arch-lords decide how to handle me? I can't prepare for the full extent of what I'll be accused of. I have no idea what domain I was in, what might be significant about it, or what false evidence the real traitors planted.

They had a scheme there that went beyond observing. If they'd only wanted to look around, they wouldn't have needed to use me as a distraction and a scapegoat. Will I be blamed for everything they did too, or are there aspects the arch-lords aren't even aware of?

It doesn't sound as if there's anyone else down here in the row of cells with me. But then, fae rarely hold their prisoners for long. On both sides of the border, we believe in swift sentencing and removal of the guilty parties to however far from the Heart their punishment requires.

I suppose that's one reason to hope I won't need to wait *too* long to find out my fate. And to try to speak up on my own behalf, if any of them will hear me.

My mind slips back to the little village and my short time there with my three men. How long have *they* been wondering about my whereabouts? Do they think I've abandoned them after all?

My stomach clenches up all over again. I glance around the cell, but there's nothing here I could use to send a message—and I doubt my jailors would allow any conjured leaf or slip of ribbon to float out of here unimpeded anyway.

I lean back against the cool stone wall and close my eyes, tuning out the sour smell seeping from the bucket as well as I can. When footsteps sound over the floor several minutes later, my heart skips a beat, but I can't tell if it's more with relief or dread.

Not one but three guards come to a stop outside my door.

"Get up," the woman in the lead snaps. "The arch-lords will interview you now. Not a single true name out of you, or you won't have a chance to yield before you're gone to dust."

I wouldn't expect anything less when it came to a supposed—and once actual—traitor to the rulers of the realm. Apparently they consider me a significant threat if they felt three warriors were necessary to escort me.

I nod in answer as I push myself to my feet. One of the other guards unlocks my door with a murmur of magical syllables. They stand back to let me emerge and then fall into formation around me, one on each side just a half a step ahead and the woman who spoke to me right at my heels.

In the past, I haven't had the chance to observe any of

the summer arch-lords' homes. I was forbidden from venturing into their domains before I ever had the opportunity to pass through. But it doesn't appear to matter which of them held me for safe keeping, because the guards march me up a short flight of stairs and right out through a side door. We head across a grassy expanse toward a building right in front of the Heart.

I haven't seen this structure before either, but I've heard it mentioned. What the summer fae call "the Bastion of the Heart," the joint building where they conduct their formal business together. It looms over the plain in gleaming radiance, veins of pure gold winding through the pale beige of the stone walls and the sharp peaks of their towers.

The gold shines even brighter than it would anywhere else because of the glowing mass right across from the building. My breath catches at the sight of the Heart of the Mists, the source of all magic within our world. The shimmering mass embedded in the hazy border between winter and summer pulses with gentle ripples of energy that wash over my skin.

I want to walk right up to it and soak in its light, but at the same time the thought strikes terror in me. What if the Heart pushes me away? I know my past actions, the way I used my magic to harm, must have tarnished me to it.

Of course, it's the opinions of the fae waiting inside the Bastion that matter most right now.

The guards lead me through one of the doors, down a narrow hall, and into a cavernous room. The ceiling rises high above my head, more gold glinting all across it and the smooth walls with their arched windows. The air feels still and cool, as do the attitudes of the three fae seated on their thrones in a semi-circle, watching my approach.

My throat constricts under their penetrating gazes. Arch-Lord Sylas's is somehow the most piercing even though one of his eyes, glazed white and scarred through starkly against his brown skin, can't be seeing anything at all. All of them look ready to dismember me if I utter a single word wrong, though.

The guards bring me to a halt before them and ease back just one step. A couple of figures lurk behind the golden thrones—members of the arch-lords' cadres, I assume.

Some part of me had been anticipating seeing Arch-Lord Corwin here as well, I realize with a sickening lurch of my heart. There's a strange, unwelcome pang of disappointment woven into my gratitude that I'm not having to look my lost soul-twined mate in the face, at least not yet.

"Lady Kara," the woman in the middle throne begins in an imperious tone, "you were brought into our custody after being apprehended in Gildrest in what appeared to be an attack on Lord Shane and his pack. Before we proceed any further into our discussion of what to do with you, we'd like to hear your account of your reasons for being there."

I swallow thickly and gather my shreds of confidence. No one could outright lie this close to the Heart without it lashing out at them visibly. They *have* to know I'm telling the truth. I just need to say it plainly enough that they can't believe I'm obscuring worse truths with my wording.

"It's a bit of a long and complicated story, so I hope you will have the patience to let me tell you everything," I say. "But to get it out of the way, I should start by making this one thing clear: I had no intention of hurting anyone living in Gildrest at the time when I was there or afterward in any possible way."

The flame-haired arch-lord lifts his eyebrows. "An odd claim from one found with many instruments of harm in her possession."

I dip my head. "Those weren't mine, and I had no idea they even existed until moments before they were found with me. But I think it would be easier for you to accept that if you let me begin my account a little earlier."

"Go ahead," Arch-Lord Sylas says. The fury underlying just those two words sends a shiver down my back. I doubt he wanted to see me go free after what I did to his mate in the first place.

I resist the urge to hug myself. "A couple of weeks ago, I became aware of a group of fae who were looking to undermine your rule and disrupt the peace treaty. I spied on them in the hopes that I could find out their plans to report them to you, but they caught me. So I pretended to want to join them, since my reputation from my past crimes would make that a plausible story."

"Or a true one," one of the lurking figures mutters from behind the thrones.

I ignore the cadre member and go on. "Once I was drawn in, I decided to continue until I had solid information I could bring to you. I knew you might find it difficult to believe me on simple hearsay, given... everything. The foray into Gildrest was meant to be my way of proving myself to the traitors so they'd give me the details of the larger plan. Obviously they didn't trust me as much as I'd believed, because they appear to have framed me for some larger crime and abandoned me there."

The flame-haired one cocks his head. "What did you believe you were going to Gildrest to do?"

"The dissidents said it was only to make some observations. They needed me to use my skill with nerves to put the guards to sleep—which I did, in a way that shouldn't have harmed them at all. Then they asked me to keep watch and simply wait. While I was doing that, one of them hit me with magic to force me closer to the castle, and another left a sack of supplies I'd never seen before near me. I'd imagine they raised the initial alarm so the pack would discover me as well."

"But you don't know," the woman says coolly.

"No," I acknowledge. "I didn't recognize any specific voice. I'm only speculating on that point. But I absolutely did not carry that sack or any of the objects in it into Gildrest, and I had no knowledge of their existence until the moment it was thrown at me. I swear in front of the Heart that I believed I would be doing nothing more to Gildrest's pack than encouraging the guards to doze off."

There is no flare of retribution. The thrum of energy in the air retains the same steady rhythm. The arch-lords exchange a glance.

Arch-Lord Sylas clears his throat. "Why would you put yourself at risk spying on or associating with these 'dissidents' in the first place? Why did you bother trying to get information? That was not a requirement of your continuing sentence."

I lift my chin. "I know. But I told you the last time I stood before you how ashamed I am of my past behavior. I know how you and so many other fae see me because of it. I hoped... I hoped I could prove that I'm not a traitor at heart. I wanted to show that I would risk as much to protect the peace now as I did to threaten it before."

The woman's eyes narrow. "You wanted to restore your reputation and your standing in society."

I suppose that's a significant part of it, but she makes the desire sound like something horribly selfish. I don't know how to defend myself against that.

As I hesitate, the muted sound of shouts carries from outside the building. The arch-lords tense, but a man comes hurrying into the room a moment later, looking harried but not panicked.

"My lords and lady," he says quickly. "Three fae have arrived who wish to speak on behalf of your current prisoner."

My pulse stutters. My men have tracked me down here? They came all this way to try to defend me?

An ache forms at the base of my throat, bittersweet because the affection swelling through my chest alongside it feels somehow hopeless.

"Which fae?" Arch-Lord Sylas demands.

The man shows a brief grimace. "I don't know the others' names, but the one who was most outspoken says he's Ronan, once of Saplight."

A cloud seems to pass over all three of the arch-lords' faces. Their gazes snap to me. "How did you come to associate with a man like *that?*" the woman asks in a voice acidic enough to burn.

My stance stiffens. Hearing her disparaging tone about one of the men I've fallen for—one of the men I'm coming to *love*, if I'm being honest with myself—angers me more than any hostility they've aimed at me.

"He isn't what you think," I say. "He took the blame to protect someone else. I'm honored that he's forgiven me for my own past crimes."

They consider me for a moment in silence. I can't tell what they make of those statements or of the flash of temper I showed.

The youngest turns to the others. "What could it hurt to hear what they have to say? At least we'll have a fuller picture."

Arch-Lord Sylas nods. The woman sighs but inclines her head as well, and the messenger lopes off again.

I feel the need to provide a little more context before they turn their questions on my men. "I happened to meet Ronan and his friends while I was traveling in the summer realm. I was injured, and they helped me. I've been staying with them in the sort-of village they've built for themselves since before I stumbled on the dissident group. They knew I was going out with the traitors last night—they'll have known something was wrong when I didn't come home."

Calling it 'home' comes so naturally I don't even realize it might sound odd until the woman's eyes twitch. But she doesn't remark on my phrasing, only stays poised elegantly in her throne with her luminescent white hair streaming over her shoulders as a couple more guards escort Ronan, Nyle, and Brice into the Bastion.

My heart wrenches at the way each of their faces brighten just slightly seeing me alive and on my feet. The woman arch-lord gestures, and my guards usher me off to the side so that the men can take my place in the center of the room.

Ronan gives me a fiercely determined look, and Brice shoots me a swift if strained smile in an attempt to be encouraging. Nyle simply holds my gaze for a few moments, but I can read the worry in his eyes.

The woman leans forward in her throne. "Let us cut to the chase. I understand that you have recently been hosting Kara of Hazeleven and that you were concerned when she went missing."

"That's correct," Ronan says with a growl in his voice. "We hoped to get news from you and learned that she was being held prisoner. Whatever crimes it appears she's committed, all of us can vouch that she was doing everything in her power to defend the Mists and the three of you, not harm you."

"And why exactly should we listen to *you*, given how much harm you've done in the past?"

Ronan's spine goes rigid. My stomach flips over. I don't expect him to betray his sister's memory now—I don't know what the arch-lords would make of it even if he did. All I can do is watch and see how this catastrophe plays out.

But he speaks, slowly and reluctantly but steadily all the same. "The harm I've done is not what I allowed my former pack to believe it was. I failed to properly protect my sister from a grievous crime being committed against her by my father, and I did not wish to sully her memory after she was gone by revealing what had happened to her. I'd prefer that this admission remain between us even now, if you'll allow that."

He glances at his friends. "I was reminded this morning by those wiser than me that the security of one living matters much more than that of one already lost."

My eyes prickle with sudden tears. I blink hard, willing them back.

"That's quite the change in story for us to simply swallow out of the blue," the flame-haired arch-lord says.

Nyle motions in the direction of the border. "The Heart obviously accepts it, or it would have shown its rejection of a lie. My friend has been punishing himself for more than three years for something that wasn't even his fault. Don't continue to punish him and the woman we're all devoted to because you're married to your old opinions."

The woman appears to bristle a bit, but Arch-Lord Sylas holds up his hand. "Regardless of what we believe about anyone's past behavior, the Heart can still show whether they're speaking genuinely on the matter at hand. We should get an account from these men and see how well it matches what we've already heard." He glances my way. "If you would welcome their testimony, Lady Kara?"

I can't hold back the sad but slightly giddy smile that crosses my lips when I gaze at my men. "There's no one I would rather have speak for me, including possibly even myself."

The guards lead me even farther away, and the arch-lords cast a dome of silence around my area of the building so that I can't hear what questions they ask or how my men respond. I suppose it's a precaution to ensure I can't direct their answers.

It means that I can't follow the conversation at all, only the passion that shows in all three men's stances and faces as they claim my innocence. The affection I felt before condenses into something almost solid coiled around my heart.

I'm not just coming to love them. I do love them, with every inch of my being. This is what it should be like, finding your mate—or mates, as the case may be. Knowing you're on the same page, that your intentions align and your hopes resonate with each other's in harmony.

Finally, the interrogation ends. The silence lifts, and my ears hum briefly with the return to normal sound. The men step aside so that my guards can escort me back into the middle of the room.

"This is all very unusual," the woman arch-lord says.

Arch-Lord Sylas is frowning. "I'm not sure, given the history we *are* dealing with, whether we shouldn't be more cautious than usual."

I look into each of their faces. "Whatever you want me to do to show I'm committed to making up for that history, just ask. I know the traitors I was spying on have something worse planned. If you'll give me the chance, I might still be able to find out what. Please."

There's a moment of tense silence. Then a voice carries from overhead—a soft, clear voice that once featured in my most rage-filled daydreams.

"Don't be ridiculous. We have to give her a chance."

22

Kara

$\mathcal{M}$y unexpected defender makes her way to the main room with uneven footsteps, one tap of her boots taking just a bit longer and falling a bit harder than the other.

As the woman walks into view with her slight limp, her slim arms folded defiantly over her chest and her dyed hair with its current mix of pink, purple, and blue flowing down her back, Arch-Lord Sylas pushes to his feet. "You said you'd only watch from upstairs."

His mate stares steadily back at him. "And you said you'd give fair judgment. The only reason you're hesitating is because of me, isn't it? So who better to put a word in?"

Then Lady Talia's gaze slides to me.

She ought to seem ridiculous with those hues that would normally only belong to true-blooded fae in her human hair, but somehow the vivid colors look perfectly right on her. She's half a foot shorter than me, and her limp is more obvious up close as she walks toward me. I know she has only the slightest bit of magic compared to what I can wield. But still I have the urge to shrink inside my skin and cower in front of her.

I hold my posture straight with all the dignity I can maintain, braced for a jolt of resentment or anger I'll need to conceal. But no hostile emotions stir inside me, not even a flicker. All that wells up in my chest is my lingering shame and undeniable respect that she's showing me more trust than any of the powerful fae around us have.

Arch-Lord Sylas makes a rough noise of disapproval, but his mate ignores him, stopping just a few feet away from me with no apparent concern that I might attack her. She offers me a gentle smile.

"I believe you," she says. "And I appreciate the risks you've taken to try to protect us and the peace. It was even more brave than it would have been if you hadn't made mistakes in the past. You had to know that you could end up here like this if things went wrong, and you could have just ignored what you'd seen and gone on with your life, but you intervened instead."

My voice comes out in a rasp. "That didn't feel like an option I could really choose."

"I can see that." Her smile softens even more. "The Heart doesn't normally choose badly. If things had turned out differently, you would have been a good mate for Corwin."

My throat closes up. I don't know what to do with all this compassion, heaped on me until I'm not sure I can hold all of it. All that tumbles out of my mouth next is a stiff, "Thank you."

Talia's mouth twists. "I'm not sure you should be thanking me. I'm only saying what's fair."

I can't stop a hint of dryness from creeping into my tone. "Not everyone seems to see it that way."

She glances over her shoulder and then returns her attention to me. "They'll get there." Then she pauses, and a trace of melancholy crosses her face. "I've also wanted to say... The last time we saw each other, the arch-lords ordered you to talk about how sorry you were. But I've never apologized to you. I'm sorry too, you know—I'm sorry I took the mate you were supposed to have."

I'm hit with another jolt of shock. My jaw drops open. I can only say, because I know how true the words are, "You didn't mean to."

"No, but it still happened, and it still hurt you more than I can imagine. So I want you to know that I'm not going to take anything more from your life, and I won't let them do it either."

She steps even closer. When I simply blink at her, uncertain but not resisting, she wraps her arms around me in a hug.

Something cracks inside me, as if her kindness has broken a dam that was pushing back a deluge. But it isn't anger that spills out, only sorrow. So much grief I bottled up from ten years ago, not wanting to let anyone, even myself, recognize how shattered I was.

A sob hitches up my throat. My eyes flood with tears. I find myself returning Talia's embrace, weeping over her shoulder.

Some distant part of me recoils from the display of emotion and flails with the urge to rein it in, clamp down on it, shut it back away. The Seelie arch-lords are seeing this, and my men, and—

But I can't find it in me to care. The woman I once saw as my greatest enemy is also the one who's shown she understands me the most, and there's something too incredible about that for dignity to matter.

Talia doesn't appear to mind my tears. She squeezes me harder as they all pour out and only backs away one step when the flood eases off. I swipe at my eyes and push back my shoulders, half expecting a fresh wave of shame, but it doesn't come. My chest feels lighter, as if I've released all that sorrow permanently.

"You know," Talia says, "the Heart makes mistakes too, and I've seen it correct them. If you appealed to it, it might give you another soul-twined bond. If it can bring someone back from the dead, it can manage that."

Somehow that possibility had never occurred to me. After what I did, I was so sure I barely deserved the bond I'd already almost had. But as the idea sinks in, I realize it doesn't matter either. And I should probably make something clear before our audience gets the wrong idea about why I've been crying.

I glance over at my men where the guards have brought them to the side of the audience room. "I wouldn't want to. *My* heart is already full with more love than I realized I was capable of feeling. I lost something ten years ago, but in just the past few weeks, I've gained so much—so much that's what I really needed."

Ronan draws his back a little straighter, and Nyle's

mouth curves into a more open smile than I've ever seen from him before. Brice has lit up like a lantern orb. I see the same conviction in all of their eyes, shining back at me.

When I tear my gaze away to look at Talia again, her smile has returned. She grasps my hand just for a second. "I'm so happy."

She means it. And in that moment, I finally know with every particle in me that Corwin and the Heart made the right choice keeping his bond with her.

Talia turns toward the arch-lords with a questioning tilt of her head as if daring them to argue with her assessment of the situation. Arch-Lord Sylas has already sunk down into his throne, looking gruffly amused. The flame-haired man's eyes are sparkling. The woman's lips have pursed, but she sighs.

"It is true that everything we've heard strongly indicates that Lady Kara meant no harm with her actions and was framed for this crime by others."

The lightness inside me expands as if my soul has taken flight. It's going to be okay.

And suddenly that makes me all the more certain that I need to see what I started through to the end, even if it's dangerous, even if I have nothing left to prove.

"If the arch-lords are willing to trust me that far," I say, "then will you also consider that we have a larger problem on our hands? I don't know why the traitors decided to set up my arrest, but they must have had a reason. We need to figure out what that was and stop whatever else they have planned. And I still want to do whatever I can to ensure they don't succeed."

Ronan lets out a growl and pushes forward. "They already turned on you once. You can't give them another chance to hurt *you*."

I shake my head at him. "They should find out that I'm not someone they can hurt and get away with it. And I'm the only one here who has any idea at all who they are and how they're thinking. Even if I don't know the specifics of their plans, I might be able to make a good guess at what they'd attempt next."

"Your help in that matter would be greatly appreciated, Lady Kara," Arch-Lord Sylas says, his voice still serious but no longer holding any anger toward me. Lady Talia has gone to stand beside his throne, and he's rested his hand companionably on her shoulder. "Unfortunately, Lord Shane hasn't reported any disruption in his domain other than what his pack found around you."

I frown. "That doesn't make any sense. They *must* have done something or taken something. Maybe he hadn't realized yet in the commotion?"

The youngest arch-lord speaks up. "Why don't we call him back in for another interview? We can have Lady Kara present in case she thinks of additional questions we should ask."

The woman nods briskly and motions to one of the cadre-chosen nearby. "Have Lord Shane return here at once."

While we wait for Lord Shane's arrival, the arch-lords pass on word to their servants, and my men and I are treated to a simple lunch at a wooden table in the field next to the Bastion. The food may not be anything fancy, but it's leagues above what I had in my prison cell, and the relief of having my innocence believed makes the mince-stuffed rolls and fruit taste even sweeter.

Ronan insists on sitting next to me and keeping his arm around me throughout the meal while he eats one-handed. Not to be completely shut out, Nyle rests his foot against mine beneath the table, and Brice reaches to touch my hand whenever it comes to rest on the table.

I find myself starting to choke up all over again. "Thank you for coming. I know it couldn't have been easy, especially for you." I glance up at Ronan.

He presses a kiss to my temple. "Losing you would have been infinitely harder."

I never thought I was the kind of woman who'd melt over a few words, but I just about do right then.

"You're my mates," I tell them abruptly, looking around at them. "All of you." Then, with an icy flicker of doubt I can't totally dismiss, "I mean, if you want to be."

Brice is already chuckling before I've finished that last sentence. He grasps my hand and holds on to it this time. "We're not going anywhere without you."

From Nyle's crooked but warm smile and the tightening of Ronan's arm around me, that sentiment is shared all around.

Part of me wishes that soaking up their affection was all I had left to do for the rest of my life, but when a messenger calls us back to the Bastion for Lord Shane's arrival, the jitter of anticipation that races through me isn't entirely unpleasant.

The dissidents double-crossed me before I could do the same to them. I look forward to making them regret it.

I didn't get a clear look at the lord before in the middle of the night and the confusion. He's a prim looking man with gray mixed into his moss-green hair. His lips curl with disdain when he sees me.

"We've determined that Lady Kara is innocent of the charges against her," says the woman arch-lord, who I've now been properly introduced to as Celia. "And that the disruption to your pack was part of a larger threat. So we'll ask you as we did before, now that you've had more time to take stock—and please do be thorough in your response: Has anything at all in your castle, the pack village, or elsewhere in your domain been altered, added, or removed since yesterday?"

Lord Shane furrows his brow as if thinking hard on the matter, but I notice that the tendons in his hands flex just for an instant as if he's holding himself back from clenching them. The question makes him tense. Because he doesn't like being imposed on again or because he already knows there's a problem?

"My pack has found no reason for concern," he says after a moment.

"And yourself?" Arch-Lord Sylas presses.

"Everything that should be there is exactly as I'd expect."

I think he answers a tad too quickly. Something about his demeanor jars against my senses, making me think of my grandfather when his nerves started to shake him.

My own question tumbles out before I can think better of it. "What about anything that *shouldn't* have been there?"

Lord Shane's head jerks toward me.

The young flame-haired arch-lord, Donovan, raises his eyebrows. "Indeed. That was very specific wording you used there. I'd like the answer to that question too."

The lord opens and closes his mouth. His face flushes with discomfort. Then he scowls. "I can't say that what is no longer there went missing last night. I hadn't looked for it in weeks."

"But there is something that *was* in a specific place the last time you checked and is no longer there as of this morning?" Arch-Lord Celia says dryly. "Something you should not have had?"

"Yes," Lord Shane admits with obvious reluctance. "I had—it was only a curiosity—one of my cousins likes to meddle with these things... It's a human weapon, one imbued with magic, which I understand is forbidden. But my family has never used it for anything, and we've kept it secured within the castle."

Arch-Lord Sylas leans forward in his throne with a grim expression. "What kind of human weapon, and what sort of magic is in it?"

The lord's throat bobs. "What they call a gun," he says faint. "A revolver, to be exact. And it was bespelled to give the shooter perfect aim at any distance. But I swear we never tried it on anything but wooden targets when we were mere whelps, not knowing any—"

The blood has drained from my face with a sudden chill. There is one thing I remember clearly from my discussions with the dissidents—and only one important figure a human weapon could pose a significant threat to.

"They want to kill Lady Talia," I burst out. "They know she was the biggest proponent for the peace—they think without her, we'll all fall back into fighting." And now they'll be able to accomplish her murder from who knows how great a distance.

My stomach sinks. They must have been counting on Lord Shane obscuring the truth to hide his illegal possession well enough that no one would realize.

All three arch-lords have turned their attention on me. I wonder if Lady Talia herself has gone back to watching from the upper level of the building.

My skin prickles, but ideas flicker through my mind, imagining what sort of plot the traitors must hope to enact —and how we might turn the tables on them.

I drag in a breath. "Isn't that one Murk arch-lord an expert at illusions? I think I might know how we could catch the traitors in the act."

23

Kara

"Wolves aren't meant to fly," Nyle mutters, peering over the edge of the carriage with uncharacteristic anxiety.

"*You* conjured the carriage," Brice reminds him in an amused tone. "You should know whether it's stable enough."

Ronan scowls at them both from the bow. "Quiet. We're up here because we want to go unnoticed. That's not going to happen if you're yammering your heads off."

"There hasn't been any sign of them yet," I say. "And we've got Arch-Lord Madoc's spell cloaking the carriage."

I'm trying to sound confident, but underneath my pulse is racing at twice its usual speed. We *are* flying much higher than fae would typically direct a carriage to go, a few dozen feet above the tops of the trees on the hilltop we're hovering over, but heights don't bother me. It's the knowledge that we're waiting for what might be our only chance to stop the traitors who double-crossed me—and are almost certainly planning murder today.

It's taken a week to put all the pieces of our plan in place. We couldn't move too quickly without risking the dissidents realizing that the arch-lords must have discovered their theft and worked out their intentions with my help.

As far as anyone knows, my three men and I were banished to the fringelands. We were even escorted on a carriage out there shortly after my trial for the benefit of anyone keeping an eye on the domains around the Heart. Then we returned by stealth.

In the meantime, the arch-lords announced a festival to be assembled in unclaimed grounds near the base of the plateau that holds their homes, to celebrate the continuing peace. No one has made any specific declarations, but they mean it to be seen as a reaction to having foiled my supposed malicious schemes. Everyone knows that Lady Talia will be there to make a speech.

The open plain where they're holding the festival will make a particularly tempting venue for anyone hoping to do her harm from a distance. And we've picked a spot with just one ideal vantage point for someone who knows they can count on certain aim even across a great distance. The terrain in the area remains flat as the grasslands give way to forest, but one low hill rises up amid the forest, giving a view over the treetops.

It's that hill we're staked out over. If the traitors are going to attempt to take a shot at Lady Talia with their stolen magic-worked gun, this will be the ideal spot—the *only* viable spot that won't bring them close to the plain and the sentries patrolling there.

I scan the patches of forest on the far side of the hill for any sign of movement. It's unlikely that the entire group will tramp onto the hilltop. They might only send a couple of fae to carry out the violence, or—I suspect—they'll have a larger plot in mind with varied tasks for many of them. We need to find out what those plans are.

With everyone believing we've been banished, we make the ideal spies. The traitors might notice if any of the arch-lords' cadre-chosen or key warriors vanish before the celebration. By all appearances, the summer fae rulers have no concern about securing the lands beyond the immediate festival area. And the illusion Arch-Lord Madoc cast around our craft should ensure no one sees or hears us up here as long as we don't move too suddenly or holler too loudly.

I murmur the true name for air under my breath, ensuring that the currents are still sweeping up and around us. I don't want even the slightest hint of our scent reaching the ground below.

Brice's expression has dimmed. He glances at me. "What if they target Lady Talia from some other spot?"

"Then they'll have to come close enough for the guards to catch them if they attempt any violence," I point out. "And they can't hurt Lady Talia anyway. She isn't even there."

It's going to be another illusion stepping onto the stage the arch-lords' people have conjured, echoing the real Lady Talia who'll be safely within one of the castles. I've brought my talents to bear to make that illusion convincing as well, taking items with her scent and encouraging the breeze to waft it through the growing crowd. If the dissidents realize she isn't really there, they'll know it's a trap.

A flicker of movement catches my eye. I twist in that direction and spot a wolf darting across a short stretch of open ground near the hill, coming from the direction of the festival. It vanishes into a narrow strip of forest, appears once more crossing a field, and vanishes into the thicker woods beyond that, just past and to the side of our hill.

The men have followed my gaze. Without any words exchanged, Ronan motions for the carriage to sink toward that area of forest. We need to find anyone else that wolf is meeting with and hear what's discussed. And I have to be closer if I'm going to work the other necessary magic that will make apprehending the traitors easier.

I speak the true name for air again, both to contain our scent and to send a gust sweeping through the trees below and up toward us. Multiple wolfish smells and one I recognize as a specific rat reach my nose.

A low growl sounds in Ronan's throat before he contains it. "The one who was lurking near our home is down there—the one we assume attacked you before we first found you."

My fingers curl around the edge of the hull. I suspected my unknown assailant was someone among the traitors, probably as unaware that it was me they'd targeted as I was that they'd done so, but having it confirmed is an uncomfortable sensation.

"We'll sort that out once they're all in custody," I say. "It doesn't really matter now."

We direct the carriage until it's right over the spot where the scents rise up thickest. I can make out several figures through the mottled shadows in a gap between the tree branches below. With another appeal to air, a continuing breeze lifts their voices to our ears.

Mohawk is with them, in the middle of making a demanding question. "—absolutely sure it's her?"

"It's hard to mistake the scent of a dung-body for anything else," a woman answers, using the derogatory term some fae use for humans. "I saw her with my own eyes too, standing to the back of the stage with her mates around her."

She must be the wolf we saw—Mohawk sent her ahead to scope out the situation. My trick worked to convince them that Talia is really there.

Despite the nervous tension thrumming through my body, a small smile crosses my lips. Brice nudges me, offering an encouraging smile of his own.

I'm using my skills in many ways today. I switch to the true name for nerves, letting the syllables slide delicately off my tongue. I'm not doing anything as intensive as putting fae to sleep right now, and a light touch is required to ensure they don't notice my meddling. All I need is for them to relax just a little, to be confident in their plans and not suspicious of the arch-lords' ulterior motives for this festival.

If they get skittish and back off now, I don't know when we'll have another chance to catch them in a treacherous act.

Mohawk barks out orders: two wolves who will keep prowling around the territory between here and the festival grounds to watch for sentries venturing farther afield, several Seelie and the Murk man who are supposed to cause different disruptions in the crowd after the shooting to add to the chaos and make the fae present believe it's an act of war between the different groups.

I switch from my focus on nerves to air again, opening a small jar of perfume as I do. It's a mix of herbal and foresty scents that shouldn't strike the fae below me as unusual if they catch a whiff, but distinctive enough that the arch-lords' people have all been instructed to be alert for it. When any of the warriors cross paths with one of the traitors, they'll know I've marked them and bring them into custody.

With soft gusts of wind, I send wisps of the scent down to attach to the hair of the fae below. They give no indication that they've noticed anything unusual as one by one they shift and set off toward the festival grounds. A little more of the tension inside me unwinds.

So far, so good.

Nyle nods in the direction of one of the wolves who's gone off to disrupt the crowd. "That's the one—the one we scented before. I'll make sure the arch-lords are aware of his additional crime."

I reach over to squeeze his arm in acknowledgment, and he presses a kiss to the side of my head.

There appears to be no one left below us except Mohawk and a woman I recognize as the patchy-haired one from her voice. "Can I do the shooting?" she asks with chilling eagerness.

Mohawk lets out a scoffing sound. "I think I'd better handle that task. Everything relies on it. Besides, I'm the one who laid my paws on the weapon so we'd have it at all."

"*I'm* the one who found out it was there," Patchy mutters, but she follows behind him as they stride through the forest toward the hill.

"Nyle had better go now," I whisper, cautious even though I know our voices should be masked.

Ronan nods and lowers the carriage at the edge of the forest. We watch until Mohawk and his companion are out of sight in the trees at the base of the hill, and then Nyle leaps out and dashes away in wolf form.

He's going to take a roundabout route to avoid the dissidents already on their way and warn the arch-lords that the plan is in motion. They have more carriages hidden under illusions, shaped for speed and ready for warriors to guide them. If all goes well, they'll be here to arrest Mohawk before the illusion of Talia ever sets foot on that stage.

The rest of us glide in the carriage back over the treetops to the top of the hill to keep an eye on Mohawk and Patchy. We're not taking any chances. Our mission isn't over until they're locked up like I was just days ago.

The trees are thinner at the top of the hill. I can see Mohawk clearly, positioning himself at the crest where he has a clear view down toward the plain. Hundreds of fae are milling around on the grassy expanse, but the stage stands out plainly, five feet above the ground. There'll be no mistaking Talia's vivid hair when she walks out onto it.

And from what Lord Shane said, as long as Mohawk

can sight her with the gun, the bullet is sure to hit her heart.

Even a fae would need swift and skilled magic to heal from such a wound. It's unlikely Talia would survive, even with the touch of the Heart on her. It's strange to think that just a decade ago, I'd have welcomed that thought. Now it only makes me feel sick.

As the minutes slip by, I force myself to watch without fidgeting. When a wolfish form appears near the base of the hill, my body tenses. But it's only one, and he has no magic on him to hide him. What's he doing?

A few moments later, he appears right beneath us, shifting into a Seelie man a few paces from Mohawk. Ronan stares down at him and goes rigid.

"What?" I murmur.

"I *know* him," he says around a snarl. "That's Gildas—one of Lady Siobhan's other cadre-chosen. He was my father's best friend."

Brice's tan skin has turned sallow. "What's he doing here? Why does he seem like he *knows* that man?"

Mohawk definitely doesn't appear to be unsettled by the visit, although he clearly wasn't expecting it.

"Shouldn't you be handling things with your lady?" he grumbles. "I thought associating with us so directly was too much of a risk to your reputation."

Gildas inhales through his teeth in a hiss. "This was too urgent to ignore. The arch-lords are attempting to trick you. It's all an illusion. But I know how you can still strike the dust-destined 'lady' down."

24

Kara

$\mathcal{A}$s the cadre-man's words ring in my ears, my hands clench around the side of the carriage so tightly my knuckles turn white. After all the precautions we've taken, all the care we've put into this plan, the ruse has been discovered after all—because our enemies have an ally closer to the arch-lords than any of us suspected. Saplight is a neighbor to Arch-Lord Donovan's domain; no doubt their people pass through and around the lands by the Heart regularly.

And now the traitors think they can still hurt Lady Talia and get away with it? What if that's true?

Mohawk has lowered the gun. Even seen from above, his scowl is deep enough to be visible. "What do you mean, 'it's all an illusion'? We checked—"

Gildas waves his hand dismissively. "They've made it a

thorough one, but Lady Talia isn't going to be appearing on that stage at all. She isn't even near it. They know about the enchanted weapon, and they're hoping to catch you in the act. You haven't seen any sentries searching out here?"

Patchy shakes her head. "We have people keeping watch. There's been no one out this far."

"Maybe they don't know how well the magic works," Mohawk suggests. "They don't think we could attack from this far away."

"That could be the case," Gildas says. "But you still need to be cautious about this."

I exchange a panicked glance with Ronan and Brice. It sounds like the Saplight cadre-man hasn't discovered enough to know that we're still in the area and helping with the arch-lords' gambit. That will work to our favor. And Nyle's warning could bring the arch-lords' warriors here before any of the rest matters.

But I still don't like this.

Gildas is motioning toward the Heart. "She wanted to watch the festival—to know how the illusion is being received. They have her in a high tower in Arch-Lord Donovan's castle where she has a clear view, with an illusion to hide her presence. You could shoot her in the window."

Mohawk growls. "Not if I can't see her. I have to be able to sight her with this weapon for the magic to work."

"Then you'll just have to disrupt the illusion momentarily at the right time," Gildas says impatiently. "I can show you a spot on Saplight's lands where you can take aim. The rest is up to you." He jerks his head toward

Patchy. "Doesn't this one have enough magic in her to buy you a second or two? That's all you'll need."

"Of course I can," Patchy snaps. "Just show us where, and we'll take care of it."

Oh, no, no, no. They're shifting into wolves now without another word.

As they dash down the slope of the hill, Ronan sets our carriage soaring after them. My pulse rattles through my veins.

Nyle will direct the warriors to the hill. I need to leave them as clear a trail as possible so they can find us from there. Please, let them be nearly here already.

I open the jar of scent again and murmur to the air. My words send tendrils of the odor gusting down to attach themselves to the underbrush along the path the traitors have taken.

"I could go ahead to Saplight," Brice says in a taut voice. "Try to speak to Mother—no, she'll be at the festival. Pretty much everyone will be. Blast it."

"You could try to find her on the festival grounds," Ronan says. "Or the arch-lords and their people—let them know they need to search Saplight's lands. Just be careful none of the treacherous mongrels catch you first."

Brice nods. I grasp his forearm with nervous fingers. "Come back safe."

He flashes me a tight smile. "I have no intentions otherwise."

As soon as we pass over a stretch of open ground, Ronan brings the carriage down so it's nearly skimming the grass. We can't afford to stop completely, or we might lose the wolves we're following. But Brice leaps nimbly over the side. He crouches low in the grass as we glide onward and take the illusion with us, waiting until there's no chance that our enemies might glance back and see him. I cast a breeze toward him to blow his scent away from them.

The traitor wolves never glance back. The pale gray one in the lead, Gildas, veers farther from the festival grounds rather than taking a straight route, presumably to avoid sentries he knows are posted.

We keep close on their tails. I conjure more wind to ripple over them and bring their scent to our noses so we can track them even when they're out of sight in the woods.

As we get closer to the vast swell of land that holds the arch-lords' domains and the Heart, Ronan's posture gets increasingly stiff. He hasn't been back to his former domain since they cast him out, valuing a dead deviant over a living hero—whether they realized that or not. It's hard for me to imagine what that must be like, seeing the familiar landscape again but not being able to consider it your own.

The wolves slow and head off even farther from the plateau. They'll need some distance to get a view of any building up top. I assume we're heading toward the edges of Saplight's territory.

Gildas leads Mohawk and Patchy up a small swell of land, lower than the hill they made use of before but more sparsely treed. When we hover over it, I can make out the upper towers of the nearest castle on the plateau.

There's no sign of vibrant hair in the two windows I

can make out, but Gildas did say an illusion would be hiding Lady Talia. My stomach clenches.

The traitors below us have shifted back into human form. "You may need to scale a tree for the best line of sight," Gildas is saying. "I believe she's in the uppermost room as that's the only one that will let her see the stage. How your colleague disrupts the illusion is up to the two of you. I'm taking my leave now before anyone notices I haven't been at the festival."

He lopes off again without another word.

Mohawk mutters something under his breath. He turns to Patchy. "Get over there however you can and send a signal when you're in place. I'll signal you back when I'm ready. As soon as I do, take down that illusion for as long as you can."

Patchy nods with a jerk and dashes away. I crane my neck, scanning the landscape around us for any sign of the arch-lords' warriors coming in our direction. There's nothing, only faint strains of music drifting all the way from the festival grounds.

"It'll take her a little time to sneak her way up there, if she manages it at all," Ronan says under his breath. "There'll be time for the guards to come."

I nod, but my lungs have constricted.

Mohawk studies the trees and picks a pine to clamber up. After a few minutes, he's settled himself onto a thick branch more than halfway up, gazing toward the castle tower. He takes out the gun and raises it, peering along its sights toward the window.

"If worse comes to worst, we tackle him," Ronan mutters. "Crash the carriage right into him if we have to.

It may be better if the guards catch him in the act, but it's best if he doesn't get the chance to hurt anyone."

"Yes," I say, swallowing thickly. "When do you think—"

I cut myself off when three figures emerge from the trees. One is Gildas, looking very peeved. Another is the raven shifter who's one of the dissidents. And held between them with blood leaking from his bashed nose is Brice.

My heart lurches. I jerk forward so quickly I might have propelled myself right over the side of the carriage if Ronan hadn't grabbed my arm. As it is, my wings shoot out and unfurl to their full potential span.

My lover stares at me for an instant, never having seen my raven features merged with my human form before, and then yanks his gaze back to the scene below.

"Your men caught this banished pack-kin of mine cutting a very urgent path toward the festival from this general direction," Gildas is saying with a sharp edge in his voice. "That seemed a bad omen, especially since I've now heard one of his friends was also stopped not far from the celebration. Have you had past dealings with them?"

My heart keeps thudding on, but the rest of me freezes to ice. Not just Brice but Nyle too. Neither of them made it to the arch-lords' people, then—neither of them managed to deliver their warning.

The arch-lords don't even know that the traitors are launching their plan, let alone from where.

Mohawk sneers down at Brice from his perch in the tree. "The banished ones? Our flighty raven princess was getting cozy with them. Somehow I don't think that's a coincidence."

Then his head jerks upward. I follow his gaze toward a brief whirl of cloud in the sky over the tower. A smile crosses his lips. "It doesn't matter. Everything is in place."

That must have been Patchy's signal that she's ready to dispel the illusion. My body goes even more rigid, but one clear thought rings through my frantic horror.

Ronan and I are now the only ones who can do anything to stop this catastrophe.

Mohawk lifts his gun, and I don't even think anymore. I simply propel myself out of the carriage and dive straight toward him.

Ronan doesn't try to hold me back this time. I hear a rustle and a thump as he must leap down as well.

I crash straight into Mohawk. We tumble out of the tree to the ground, a quick flap of my wings keeping me from hitting the earth hard enough to injure me.

Unfortunately, that means he isn't knocked too badly either. He kicks me and swings at my head with the side of the gun. I try to dodge, but the metal surface glances off my forehead, sending a stabbing pain through my skull.

But raven "princesses" are trained to fight too. I punch him in the nose like his man did to Brice and slam my elbow into his wrist. The gun slips from his grasp and lands a few feet away by the roots of a tree.

In the other direction, Ronan has pinned down Gildas in wolf form. A roar of fury reverberates from his throat. As I struggle with Mohawk, the older man's desperate voice splits the air.

"Please! I yield. Just say what you want. I—I can see that Lady Siobhan pardons you. I can tell them what your father was doing, why you attacked him—I can clear your name."

A different sort of horror rushes through me even as I fend off Mohawk's blows and attempts to shove me off him. This man, this friend of Ronan's father, *knew* what the man was doing and never said anything. Not when he could have helped Ronan's sister, and not when Ronan was banished.

I want to hurl myself off Mohawk and tear my talons into that shameful excuse for a fae. But Ronan has him— and maybe Ronan would accept that. This could be his chance to ensure his welcome home.

It's easier not to want something if you don't think you can have it anyway.

In my momentary distraction, Mohawk thrusts me to the side. I roll and spring back onto my feet, ready to lunge at him. He jumps up too, poised to fight.

I'm slightly closer to the gun. His gaze twitches between me and it as he appears to debate whether he needs to take me down before it's worth making a grab at it. Then his gaze briefly slides to his ally.

Ronan has transformed back into a man, his still-clawed hand clamped around Gildas's throat with his claws digging in. His teeth are bared to reveal the wolfish fangs he hasn't retracted either.

"I don't give a rat's ass about regaining anyone in Saplight's good opinion," he snarls, his entire massive frame shaking with rage. He finally has an appropriate target to direct his vast stores of anger at. "And with what you just said, it's going to take quite a yield before I'm satisfied."

I shift my weight on my feet, my gaze flicking back to Mohawk. My wings flex over my back.

The leader of the dissidents glares at me. Then, so fast I can hardly track the movement, he snatches a dagger I didn't realize he had in his pocket and whips it at me.

I fling myself out of the way, and the blade rakes across my wing, sharp enough to cut through the feathers and sever the thin flesh beneath. As the pain stabs through my limb all the way to my shoulder, Mohawk pounces on the gun.

He grasps the weapon in his now-wolfish jaws and bounds toward the tree. With a few swift springs, he's landed on his chosen branch again. As he shifts back, he casts an answering cloud into the sky to signal his collaborator. Then he aims the gun at Lady Talia's window.

"No!" I scream out.

I heave myself upward, gritting my teeth against the agony in my one wing. I register his finger curling around the trigger, but I don't care. I don't care that her end could mean the reforming of my bond. I don't care that I could meet a fate as dire as he intends for her.

If it comes down to the blast of a bullet, then better it catches me than her. I tried to steal her life once, and now I can give it back.

And if this is the end of me, then at least… at least I got to have a taste of real happiness before I reached it. What I've had is worth more than any unknown bond.

I hurtle toward Mohawk. As he squeezes the trigger, I

sweep my wings as hard as I can for one last burst of speed.

The gun sparks, and the bullet slams into my chest.

The pain before is nothing compared to this moment. It's as if I'm being seared open from my shoulder to my gut. I grasp at Mohawk and manage to snag my fingers around his arm, yanking him with me as I plummet.

As we careen toward the ground, I get a glimpse of Gildas's gray wolf wrenching away from Ronan's hold toward us as if to help his co-conspirator. But Ronan practically flies himself, lunging after his former pack-kin.

His claws rip through Gildas's throat so deep they must scratch the spine. Scarlet liquid spurts across pale fur.

I hit the ground with my vision hazing red both with agony and another fae's blood.

Mohawk has shifted too. His jaws snap at my neck—

And a third wolf with Brice's tawny coloring slams into him, knocking him off me.

Without giving my attacker a chance to yield, Brice shifts. He snatches up the dagger that cut me from where it fell and plunges it right into Mohawk's heart.

I blink, the world going hazy around me. The pain is radiating through my lungs, turning my pulse sluggish. I have nothing left to hold on to.

Nothing except the faces of two of the men I love as they appear above me.

"Stay with us," Brice urges, and mumbles true name after true name as he hovers his hands over my chest.

Ronan spins, maybe thinking to run for help, but just then several figures come charging into the clearing.

"What happened?" the auburn-haired man in the lead demands, and I vaguely recognize him. "We heard shouts and then the shot—I thought—"

"Their plans changed," Ronan interrupts, jabbing his hand toward me. "Do any of you have healing skills? She took the bullet meant for Lady Talia."

The auburn-haired man dashes to my side and crouches down. Up close, his golden eyes spark a clearer sense of recognition. He's one of Talia's other mates, from Arch-Lord Sylas's cadre.

There's no sign that he rejoices the pain I'm now in on her behalf. He sets his hand over my wound and murmurs several emphatic words.

The pain begins to numb, and my lungs unlock enough for me to drag in a shaky but full breath.

"Thank you," he says in a low voice, sounding a little shaky himself. "It's okay now. You're going to be okay."

He says it like that's a good thing. Like he wants to keep me in this world. And if even one of the mates of the woman I once tried to murder can believe that I deserve to be okay...

I can believe it too.

25

Three years later

Kara

I know I've stood too long staring at the dresses in my wardrobe when Nyle comes up behind me and wraps his arms over mine.

"I don't think the arch-lords care that much what you've got on as long as it's decent," he says with arch amusement.

I push my fingers back through my hair and lean into his embrace. "I just want them to see how well we're doing. This was kind of an experiment. I should look like a proper lady."

A hint of a heated growl creeps into his voice as he

dips his head to nuzzle the side of my neck. "You're never anything less than a lady, darling raven. And I think there's plenty of evidence that our 'experiment' is working out very well."

His hands slide down to the swell of my belly, small but noticeably grown in the past four months since my mates and I realized I was expecting. A giddy flush washes over my skin at the thought of the family we'll soon be starting—expanding the family that we already are.

We had no idea how long it might take for us to have a child, or if it would happen at all. For many fae it takes decades if not centuries. When we first noticed the seed had taken hold, Brice beamed at me and said, *The Heart has shone on us.*

And I think that's true. The power at the core of our world took something away from me once, but it hasn't shied from offering me wonders as well.

Including the fact that I'm still here at all, though that may be more luck than divine intervention. In the mirror on the wardrobe door, I can see the scar just over my own heart poking from beneath my underslip amid the true-name marks.

The gun that delivered that wound no longer exists, melted down through magic until it was nothing more than a blob of metal. The scent I laid down led the arch-lords' warriors to most of the dissidents at the festival and allowed them to free Nyle, and enough of those traitors turned on their own group to unearth several more. In the years since, there've been no more signs of organized unrest within the Mists.

And shortly after, the arch-lords and Lady Talia held a

public ceremony in which they gave me and Ronan a formal pardon, confirmed all three of my beloved men as my mates—and established the site of the men's makeshift village as an official domain with me as its lady.

Technically, none of my men can be considered lord of the home we now call Breezehaven, because none of them are true-blooded. If we were being traditional about it, I'd have to call them my cadre. But as far as I'm concerned, they have just as much authority here as I do, and the folk of our growing community refer to them all as "Lord" anyway, without much concern for custom. We aren't the sort of domain where strictness is seen as a virtue.

And there won't be any "true" lord in Breezehaven while I rule here. I have all the mates I need.

Ronan prowls into the room, looking so stunning in his embroidered tunic and fitted trousers that my mouth starts to water. He doesn't often dress up in formal clothes, but they suit him so well.

He catches my look and grins with the relaxed warmth that's come so much easier to him after his last encounter with his former pack. There've been no more outbursts of temper or violent nightmares since then.

He swoops in for a kiss, but there isn't time for more than that. Guessing my problem, he swivels toward the wardrobe and plucks out a dress seemingly at random. "This one."

I glower at him, but when I pull it on to humor him, I find I agree. The indigo fabric brings out the coolly vivid hues in my dark hair, and the gold filigree along the hems and waist adds a summery touch to the otherwise wintery color.

"There," Nyle says with a chuckle. "You're perfect."

It feels like I've barely had time to step into my shoes before one of our folk is calling up from outside: "The delegation is arriving!"

We hurry down the staircase of our castle of earth, bronze, and gold and catch up with Brice in the clearing outside. Most of the folk of Breezehaven have come out of their houses—some similar earth-and-metal constructions that he and Nyle constructed together, others of varying materials that their owners conjured to their liking.

Tisdoe, the raven woman who's taken over most of the cooking duties for any kind of event, has laid out a spread of snacks and drinks on a table at one side of the clearing, her wolf and rat assistants beside her. Eager murmurs travel through the small crowd—curious, excited, and a little nervous too.

I can relate to all of those emotions. It was plenty of turmoil just welcoming my parents and grandfather for a brief visit earlier this year, as delighted as I was to see Grand-da. Having the rulers of our lands coming to call is another order of magnitude entirely.

A carriage glides into view along the forest path we've expanded as we also expanded the village grounds to accommodate our growing community. I spot Lady Talia's bright hair at once where she's perched near the bow with two of her mates right behind her. It's mainly the summer arch-lords who've come to call on us, since our domain is in their realm, but representatives for the Unseelie and the Murk have joined the delegation as well.

Nothing stirs in my chest at the sight of Arch-Lord Corwin's handsome face other than happiness that he felt comfortable making this visit. We've all ended up in the places that are best for us.

I step forward to meet the carriage as it glides to a stop at the edge of the clearing and the passengers disembark. "Welcome, Lady Talia, Arch-Lords Sylas, Celia, Donovan, Corwin, and Madoc." When two other figures hop out behind the others, a wider smile touches my lips. "Welcome, Whitt and August of Hearth-by-the-Heart."

August, Arch-Lord Sylas's cadre-chosen who healed my bullet wound, catches my eyes with a smile in return and a dip of his head.

"It's an honor to host you all," Ronan says from where he's come up beside me, his voice a little gruff.

Brice balances him out with typical sunniness. "We can give you a tour of the place to show you everything we've set up. And all of our kin are eager to help you feel at home."

As we lead the lordly procession around the village, our folk prove him right with murmured welcomes and awed smiles. Several offer tokens of their work to Lady Talia, who accepts them with a faint blush as if she isn't totally sure she deserves that kind of fawning.

It occurs to me in a way it hadn't quite before that she must have had even more trouble finding her footing in this fae world of ours and becoming sure of herself than I ever did. I only met her after she was already hailed as a beloved savior, but she didn't start there.

Arch-Lord Corwin exclaims over the cold-sauna Brice finished long ago with admiration for the concept. "A little taste of winter here in the middle of summer. That's brilliant."

Brice grins at me. "I had excellent inspiration."

"Even some of us wolves have found it enjoyable for short stretches," Nyle remarks. "But a little winter goes a long way when it comes to the climate."

I give him a subtle swat, and he shoots me a quick smirk.

The two Murk musicians who joined our community several months ago start playing a light but spirited melody. The delegation ends up gathering by the refreshments table, and for a time there's not much conversation other than compliments over the spread of food and drink. Ronan lights up with pride when normally stern Arch-Lord Celia practically swoons over the cheese from his goats' milk and asks him if he can start sending some of the extra supply all the way to her home in Tumble-by-the-Heart.

Licking crumbs off her fingers, Lady Talia turns to take in the village again. She glances at me. "How many have joined your—what do you call it, when it's not exactly a pack?"

One corner of my mouth quirks upward. "It's not exactly a flock or a colony either. We don't want anyone to feel excluded, so we simply refer to each other as our folk. That seems to work well for everyone. And there are eighteen of us now."

"Every few months, one or two more turn up," Ronan says. "It seems there are always more fae who don't quite fit in anywhere except a place where none of us entirely fit."

"It's a wonderful community you've assembled here," Arch-Lord Donovan says with genuine warmth. "I'd like to see more villages like this springing up, fully integrating all fae instead of just one or two odd ones out."

Arch-Lord Madoc cocks his head. "I'm sure more fae will take this place as a model to imitate as everyone gets more used to the peace."

Arch-Lord Sylas raises his cup. "I hope it'll be so. To the peace!"

"To the peace," we all echo with a clinking of glasses, and a little light glows inside me with the thought that we've kept that peace in part thanks to me.

By the time the delegation leaves, I'm happy but exhausted. My mates escort me up to the large bedroom that's theoretically mine but very often shared by all.

I flop onto the expansive bed, and they cuddle in around me, enveloping me in their warmth.

"No twinges of regret about the elevated life you could have had among the arch-lords?" Nyle says in a tone that's all teasing.

I snort and snuggle deeper into the nest of their bodies. "None at all. I have everything I could possibly want."

I feel Ronan's smile against my temple, followed by the rumble of his voice. "So do we."

And I drift off to sleep, knowing right down to the core of my being that I am exactly where I'm meant to be. My soul could not be twined more with any place or anyone than it is with the home and the mates I chose.

Want to spend more time in the world of the Mists? Check out the Bound to the Fae series for the full story of Talia's unexpected romance with her fae men, her role in the war with the Murk, and how her life and Kara's collided.

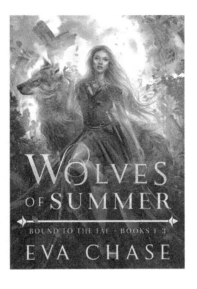

Scan the code to find it on Amazon or visit
https://mybook.to/BttFset1

ABOUT THE AUTHOR

Eva Chase lives in Canada with her family. She loves stories both swoony and supernatural, and strong women and the men who appreciate them. Along with the Bound to the Fae series, she is the author of the Heart of a Monster series, the Gang of Ghouls series, the Flirting with Monsters series, the Cursed Studies trilogy, the Royals of Villain Academy series, the Moriarty's Men series, the Looking Glass Curse trilogy, the Their Dark Valkyrie series, the Witch's Consorts series, the Dragon Shifter's Mates series, the Demons of Fame Romance series, the Legends Reborn trilogy, and the Alpha Project Psychic Romance series.

Connect with Eva online:
www.evachase.com
eva@evachase.com

Printed in Great Britain
by Amazon

23706481R00142